Down to the Creek

HEATHER MORRIS

ISBN: 1493576011

ISBN-13: 978-1493576012

ACKNOWLEDGMENTS

First and foremost I want to thank God for fabricating these characters and story lines and allowing me the creativity to get them done. Thank you to my family and friends for being so patient with me while I was immersed into these storylines. And a very special thank you to those family and friends that helped me proof the books by reading them and giving such good information back! Couldn't get them published without you!

1

Lying back on this creek bank looking up at the clouds moving above, hearing the creek water rush by and listening to the birds chirping in the trees is one of my favorite past times. Ever since I was about five years old, my father has been bringing me here to fish and take pictures. He taught me how to use the camera and lit the fire I now have blazing inside of me for photography.

I just graduated from Colvin High School here in Colvin, Oklahoma and I leave tomorrow for Los Angeles where I am enrolled at UCLA. I am so excited to get out of this small town in the middle of nowhere and move to a place full of life. I want so badly to get out of this town that I will be leaving earlier than most college students.

My only hang up about leaving would be leaving my best friend Aiden. My father has been the head foreman on Aiden's family's ranch for around many, many years and once I was old enough he brought me around and I instantly fell into a close friendship with one of the owner's sons that was the same age as I was. We have been to this creek so many times that I have a hard time picturing him not being here too. I'm going to miss him terribly but can't wait to get out of here at the same time.

That would be why I am chilling out by myself on the bank today. I'm struggling with how to say goodbye to Aiden. Just seeing his face when I leave is going to kill me. I want him to be more than my best friend, but he doesn't feel the same. Maybe I should ask him to come with me, but he's going to college in Tulsa at the end of the summer. It would be the perfect scenario for me to have Aiden and LA at the same time. If only.

We r going tubing at 5. U in?

Text from Savannah. She has been my next door neighbor since 4th grade. She is really the only girlfriend that I have been close to. Tubing? Who goes tubing? Why would you want to sit on a tube with your butt in the water and creep down the river when you can sit here on the bank and fish?

Not sure.

I have never really done much with friends because of the studying I have had to do to get my full ride scholarship to UCLA. I knew I had to work extra hard to leave here.

Come on. Everyone is going. Last time all 2gether.

Should I go? I guess it will be the last time to see everyone before I leave… Oh why not? Please tell me I won't regret this.

Sure, meet you at your house in 30. At the 6AB.

****

"Hey Karlie, you ready?" asks Savannah as she opens the front door. "Just need my sunscreen."

"Yep. Let's get this over with." I say as I let out a long sigh. She looks at me and rolls her eyes.

"You will love it, I promise." Savannah says and gives me a big hug with a huge smile on her face. Her smiles always seem to help her get whatever she wants. She is a force to be reckoned with.

I hope I don't regret this. I did wear my favorite black bikini that I have never let anyone see me in. Goodness maybe I shouldn't be doing this... When I get to LA everyone will be wearing these so I better get used to it. Savannah has on a skimpy pink one so I won't be alone with not much on. But everyone is going to be staring at me. Too late to change my mind and turn back?

Too late now. This is going to be horrible. What was I thinking? Was I thinking?

Just as I predicted everyone is staring at us as we walk towards the group. That group includes Aiden and his older brothers Austin, Aaron and little sister Audrey. Audrey's best friend Tracey, along with a bunch of others I know from school, are also here. I realize I am standing here alone while Savannah is making out with her boyfriend Jordan. Great. I probably look dumb and out of place. Everyone is looking at me as if they have seen a ghost. Maybe I do look ridiculous. Why did I decide to do this?

****

"Hey Aiden, did you invite Karlie?" asks Austin from across the pickup. "You two are attached at the hip most of the time."

"Funny, brother. She is always studying and never has time to do anything fun like this. So, no I didn't." I say quickly as I grab our tubes and head for the water.

"Well little brother, maybe you should have, look at that." Austin says as he and the rest of the crowd turn toward a car that pulled up. I look knowing it is Savannah's car and start to turn away when I spot a second girl that seems familiar but new.

Out comes Savannah and oh my, is that Karlie? Can't be. I have never seen her in anything except a one piece bathing suit with shorts. This girl has on a black bikini and her hair is down and whirling around her shoulders in the breeze. Holy cow she is gorgeous. That can't be the Karlie Mae that I have known and loved my whole life. But it is.... Whoa!!! I look around and see how everyone is also stunned by her. To change the awkward silence I walk towards her.

"Karlie Mae, is that you?" I ask with a whisper. "I can't believe you're here!"

"Yep, it's me. Hi, Aiden. Savannah thought I should come and have one last bit of fun before I leave for LA." Karlie says a little shakily. "I didn't know you were going to be here but I'm glad you are so I won't have to do this alone." She looks so uncomfortable.

"Well, you look great and I'm glad you're here. Let's go. You can use one of my tubes." I say trying not to show the uneasiness in my voice. I want to get her in the water so that the rest of the guys can't look at her in that tiny piece of material any longer.

****

Aiden is acting weird today. Maybe I look as ridiculous in this bikini as I feel. I should have worn a shirt and shorts over it. What was I thinking? Although, floating on this river is pretty fun. I should have come and done this with them long before now.

Aiden has always asked me to come with him but I was too busy studying that I passed up everything fun. Until now I never really thought I was missing out on anything.

Aiden looks so hot though with only swimming trunks on. His muscles from working on the ranch, oh my. What would it feel like to have those arms wrapped around me or those lips touching mine? I will never know. Snap out of it! Daydreaming about your best friend is uncalled for.

After about an hour I say, "Aiden how far do we go? This is really fun. Wish I would have come before now." Feeling relaxed and content, I lay my head back and look up at the clouds. I really should have come and done this years ago.

"We go to the bridge on the far side of old man Ryder's farm. Usually takes a couple of hours. I always asked you to come with me, you were too busy shoving your nose in a book!" he says and splashes me right on the front of my body soaking me to the core.

I squeal and splash him back and of course upset my tube, dumping myself fully under the water. Getting over the shock of the cold water on my bare skin I feel arms wrapping around me and pulling me to the surface. I gasp for a breath as I surface and frantically reach for my tube which of course has floated on without me. I look around for somewhere that I can touch the bottom. I never have been good at the whole treading water thing.

Luckily, Aiden has kept a hold of his tube and I realize it was his strong arms wrapped around me. My face had to have turned bright red with the embarrassment of what just happened. From dumping myself in the creek to knowing his arms were wrapped around me. Skin to skin. I have always wondered what it would be like to have them around me, but never under these ridiculous circumstances. How embarrassing. He must think I am a nit wit.

I allow him to help me to the creek bank and hear him yell to the others to go on ahead. I get out of the water fully aware that all I have on is this wet skimpy suit. Thank goodness the top stayed on during my plunge. I try to cover myself and turn to see him staring at my body in a very strange way. That look makes me try to cover myself even more.

"Why are you looking at me like that? Do I have mud on my face or what?" I ask fully annoyed at this point. And very uncomfortable again.

"Um not on your face no." he says and comes nearer and tries to wipe off the mud that is on my hip and stomach. Having his hands on my skin is driving me slowly insane. I can't take any more and push his hands away and walk towards the vehicles we had left behind. I have to put some space between us before I make a complete fool of myself, even though it's a long walk. Why didn't I wear my shorts and t-shirt?

****

Oh my goodness Karlie is so hot. I couldn't help but try to brush the mud off of her body. Just being able to touch her is such a rush. It took all I had not to let my hands wander any farther. Then she pushed me away and rushed off. I shouldn't have done that. She must think I am a creep now. Way to go Aiden. Your chance to touch her and you scare her away like a creep.

"Karlie, what's wrong? Are you okay? Did you swallow too much water?" I ask as I walk towards her at a quicker pace to catch up seeing her shake her head no but hearing no words. I continue to walk behind her trying to understand what just happened.

"Karlie Mae, what is wrong? Talk to me." At this point I step in front of her forcing her to look at me. "What's wrong?" We have made it back to the vehicles and I see mine in the distance. I don't want this day to end but I know she is mad at me.

"Nothing Aiden, when will everyone else be back?"

"Not sure but I have some water in the cooler if you want some. And I probably have jerky in there too if Audrey hasn't eaten it all." I say and head to my pickup to give us a little distance that she obviously thinks we need. It would be so easy for me to just wrap my arms around her and show her just how I feel about her but just touching her to rub off mud sent her on a dead run the other way.

"Thanks." She says as I hand her a water bottle and a piece of jerky. I know it's her favorite kind and I hope it scores a few points back into her good graces.

"Are you sure you're okay?" I ask hoping to actually get her to speak to me. "I didn't mean to make you tip over. I was just goofing around."

"I know it was my own dumb fault. Don't worry about it. I just need to get home as soon as Savannah gets back. Have a lot of packing left to do." She says and turns her back to me again and watches for the others. I let my tailgate down and offer her a spot on the other end.

"So, you're leaving tomorrow huh?" I ask trying to make small talk but knowing the answer is yes.

"Yes."

"I'm going to miss you. The creek won't be the same without you." I say turning away because I know the emotion is too close on this subject. As I do I see the group running towards us.

As the group reaches us, Savannah yells out, "Hey Karlie, can you get a ride home? I think I'm going to stay awhile with Jordan. Do you mind?"

"She can go with me Savannah, no worries" I say handing my siblings their towels and taking their tubes from them. "I'm going by her house anyway."

"Thanks Aiden, see you later Karlie! Don't forget to stop by and say goodbye before you leave tomorrow." Savannah yells as she runs to Jordan.

****

Great. I told him I have a ton of packing to do but I really don't want to go home where my parents are so upset about my leaving. They make me feel guilty for having dreams away from here even though I tell them I will come and visit as often as I can.

"You ready Karlie? Let me put these tubes in the back of Austin's pickup and then I will take you home in mine." Aiden declares as he lifts the tubes into the back. Once again I am struck with how hot he is.

"I really don't want to go home though Aiden. Mom has been sad and weepy all day about me leaving."

"Well, let's go to the creek. Poles are in the bed of the pickup and a blanket in the backseat." He says and smiles broadly knowing I won't argue with that.

"It will be getting dark before long though, Aiden. We've never been out there after dark." I say slowly, knowing that I want nothing more than to spend more time with him.

"I have kerosene lamps in the toolbox still from Austin and I having to camp out in the pasture with a sick calf yesterday." He says with a big smile. "We can stop and get the stuff to make S'mores. I know you love them."

"Fine. Let's go." I say reluctantly. This might be fun though I won't let Aiden know that. This may be the last time I see him. I guess this will be our way of saying goodbye. How do I do that? How do I tell the best person in my life goodbye?

"Karlie, are you ok?" Aiden asks with concern. "You zoned out. What's going on in that pretty head of yours? Are you still freaking out about earlier?"

"Nothing, let's go." I say quickly not wanting to get back into all that mess.

****

Once we pull up to our spot at the creek I start to get butterflies in my stomach and see that it is getting dark. I have never thought I could be out here like this with Karlie.

My brothers have brought girls here all the time, but I never have because it's mine and Karlie's special spot. I couldn't bring anyone but her here. Now is my chance.

I get out and gather up the blanket, lamps, and poles. I hand the blanket to Karlie and watch her slowly spread it out and make sure it's perfect. She seems nervous to be here. I wonder if it's me she is nervous to be around. I lay down and pat the spot next to me watching her reluctantly lay down too. I put my arm under her head like we have done since we were little and feel her roll towards me.

Lying on this blanket looking at the stars with Karlie has got to be heaven. How do I say goodbye to her? She is my best friend and the love of my life. I just wish I were brave enough to tell her. But she leaves in the morning. What a mess. I have to do something to get my mind off of all this. So I retrieve my arm and stand.

"I'm going for a swim, wanna join?" I ask hoping for a yes and start undressing...

"It's going to be chilly, Aiden." She says with a look on her face showing just how crazy she thinks I am.

"Oh come on Karlie Mae, live a little." I say knowing she hates me calling her by her middle name.

"Don't call me that!" she says. "Let's go, you talk too much." And with that she follows me into the water.

We don't get in very far I start to think I am as crazy as she thought. The water is pretty cold. She was right. Bad idea. She is shivering and I believe I am too. "Ok Karlie you win, it's too cold!" I say quickly and start for the bank.

She has already started up the bank when she stumbles and falls back towards the water. I instinctively reach out and catch her. Before I know it I have my arms wrapped around her tiny waist and she has her hands on my chest. She feels so good in this position. Her skin is so soft. I wish I could keep her just like this forever. She fits so naturally. I want to kiss her more than I have wanted anything in my life. As I look down at her, she is looking up at me with those gorgeous green eyes that melt my heart.

She is looking at me and licking her lips. I have got to taste those lips. This may be my last chance before she leaves tomorrow. I bend my head with the intent to kiss Karlie but I can't help pause just before touching her lips. As I do she rises up and meets my lips with hers.

It's like fireworks are going off around us as our kiss continues and my feelings begin to surface. I love this girl with all that I am and this is the last chance I have to show her that.

I wrap my arms tighter around her waist and she goes up on tip toes to put her arms around my neck. I try to deepen the kiss and run my tongue over her bottom lip. She opens her mouth and we lose all track of where we are and I even forget who I am. I have wanted to do this for as long as I can remember.

Karlie presses herself against my body and I feel even more fireworks. Her body is so soft where mine is strong and hard. She fits against me as if we were made for each other. This is the best feeling in the world. Kissing her is the best thing I have ever experienced. I love her so much.

I walk her backwards towards the blanket and slowly lay her down while she looks up at me with all the trust and love I am trying to convey to her. Could she really feel the same for me? Why have I waited so long for this moment? Are we really ready for this?

I hope we know what we are doing. This can't be undone. But I can't stop touching her either. And the noises she is making. I hope she knows how much I love her.

****

"Karlie, are you okay?" I hear Aiden ask as I lay here looking at the stars wondering what we just did. "Karlie talk to me please."

"Aiden, I have to go. Please take me home." I say with too much emotion and quickly get up and search for my clothes.

I stand up and start dressing. I can't believe I just slept with my best friend. The one person I have always been able to count on. The one man I will love for eternity. What have I done? He looked at me with so much love and I have waited forever to see that from Aiden but what about LA? If I let this go any further, will I be stuck here in Colvin? I can't be stuck here. And Aiden isn't LA material... Oh goodness what have I done? How could I let this happen? It was amazing and the most wonderful thing that has ever happened to me but maybe the worst thing to happen to my future. I have to get out of here. But no car. Great. He is my only chance of escape.

"We haven't even made S'mores. But ok, let's go." He says reluctantly and dresses too. We pick up all the gear and head to his pickup.

As I climb inside, I see regret on his face. I can't look at him anymore. How could I let myself get carried away like that? He will never look at me the same way again. He probably thinks of me as a little sister and here I go and sleep with him. What was I thinking? I wasn't, that's the issue.

"Thanks for the ride, Aiden." I say as I climb out and run to my front door with tears in my eyes after the long car ride in silence. I didn't know what to say and I didn't want to make him feel any worse. And I sure couldn't feel any worse.

I can hear him calling my name but I ignore him and escape inside. Inside where no one can see me cry because I just had the most amazing experience that may turn out to be the worst.

I go to my room and finish packing. All I can do is leave for LA. My flight leaves midafternoon but I think I'll get a start on it now and hopefully get out of here as early in the morning as I can before anyone realizes. Mom and Dad will understand. But will Aiden? How do I leave him? How do I stand face to face with him again?

****

"Honey, are you ready?" asks Dad bright and early. "We can get going when you are. You're sure you don't want to say goodbye to anyone? The plane doesn't leave for hours; we really don't have to leave this early."

"Savannah is on her way but that's it. Thanks Dad. You can take my luggage. Just give me a minute in here." I say sadly fighting back tears. I am supposed to be happy. I have been dreaming of leaving here for years. Worked so hard to be able to. So why do I feel so terrible?

As I look at all the pictures I have taped to my door I see Aiden in so many of them. Fishing at our spot and riding his favorite horse Spook. I sigh and know I have to leave. I can't see him again or I will fall apart making a fool of myself like I did last night at the creek. I can still feel his lips on mine.

I take a picture down of Aiden and myself at the creek and kiss it. "Goodbye Aiden. I will always love you." I say as the tears begin to form in my eyes. I put the picture in my wallet and head for the door.

"Ready to go Hollywood?" Asks Savannah as I enter the living room.

"Sure thing, doll." I say with a forced smile before hugging her tightly. Aiden isn't the only one I am going to miss.

****

She just ran away from me. Was I that bad? I know this was my first time but it was hers too, I thought. Maybe not. I saw so much hurt and regret on her face during the drive back to her house. How could I have done that to her? She is leaving and now she will never come back if she is ashamed of what we did. And of me…

As I drive to Karlie's house I keep replaying everything that happened last night in my head. I have called and texted her at least twenty times this morning but she won't answer. I have to catch her before she leaves or I will never have another chance to tell her how I feel.

But when I pull up at her house I can see her Mom's car is gone and my heart sinks. I missed her. Was she that ashamed she left earlier than planned? She didn't love me at all. How could she just leave without a goodbye?

I slam my hand on top of the steering wheel and realize that maybe last night was a goodbye....

Feeling about as down as I have ever felt, I walk into the barn to see Dad and Austin saddling up two horses. They must be going for a ride to check the sick calf in the far pasture. Not sure that I feel like talking I turn away hoping they didn't see me enter in the first place.

"Aiden, what's up? Not even going to say hello?" Dad says and walks towards me and hands me the bridle he was about to put on his horse.

"Sorry I'm just not in the mood to talk. Are you going out to check on the calf?"

"Yep. You want to go with us Son? Whatever has you so down will seem small once you get out there and see the views and expanse of land before you."

"I'll get Spook for you if you do Aiden." Austin says and starts towards my horse's stall. Should I go or stay? Maybe a ride in the fresh air will help clear my head.

"Sure. Well, if you are going to go, I don't need to. I can finish up the feeding before I head over to the nursery." Austin says and takes the saddle back off his horse. He almost seems relieved to not have to go back out there again.

"Ok, Aiden and I will go."

After saddling my favorite horse I see Dad start towards the pasture gate on the north side of the barn. We are going the long way I see. Great he is going to want to pry what is bothering me out. Can I still get out of this? No, he needs my help. And I need to think of something other than Karlie.

"So, Son what is on your mind this early in the day? I saw you left bright and early but wasn't gone long."

"I went to talk to Karlie before she left."

"Oh today was the day she was leaving for UCLA right?"

I just nod my head and look away. I really can't rehash this right now. My heart is broken and I feel like I could just weep like a little baby.

"Son, you have known for a couple of months that she was leaving. You should have been prepared to tell her goodbye."

"That's the problem Dad, she left before I could tell her anything. She just left."

"Wow, that doesn't sound like Karlie. You two have been inseparable since you were children."

"I know that's why it hurts so much. She didn't care enough to even say goodbye to me. I thought I was her best friend."

"You are going to have to make a choice then Aiden. Either you sit around wallowing in the pain and waste your life or you look out over this ranch that has been in our family for generations and realize that this is your future. You just graduated and now it's time for you to go off to Tulsa to college and then come back and claim what's yours here. That is what you still want isn't it? Or do you want to go to LA with Karlie?"

"Go to LA? I never even thought of that Dad. I know what I'm supposed to do; I just miss her so much. I knew it was going to be hard to see her go, but not seeing her or talking to her is worse. I just can't believe she left without even a word."

"That is strange. I'm sorry Son. Do you want me to call Gene and see what he says? Maybe he can shed some light on the subject." He then starts to dial the number.

"Hey Gene, it's AJ. Oh no, everything is ok here on the 6AB, that's not what I was calling about. Aiden just got back from your house where he thought he would be able to see Karlie before she left for LA but you guys were already gone. Yes, he did go to your house. No, he is back here now. Said you were gone and she didn't call or let him know she was going earlier. No, he said he hasn't talked to her. Didn't say goodbye. Kinda what I thought too. Strange kids these days. Ok, drive safe my friend. See you later."

"Well, Gene said Karlie was up very early and ready to leave. Said she had already said all the goodbyes she was going to say. Are you sure you didn't talk to her maybe last night? I thought I saw your pickup going towards the creek."

"I'm sure. We went out there because she didn't want to go home yet after we went tubing. She said her parents were upset she was leaving. When I dropped her off she didn't say her plans had changed. Dad, I don't get it."

"Aiden, what happened between you two last night? Did you have a fight or something?"

"No, we didn't fight. I'm going to call her again." I dial her number but it goes straight to voicemail. "Dad, she always answers when I call. What is going on?"

"Son, it sounds to me like she wants to put a little distance between you two. More than just the mileage between here and LA. You need to either go to LA and make her talk to you or just move on with your life and don't dwell on this anymore. It's your call Aiden."

I pull my phone back out and decide to send her one last text. If she doesn't answer this one, then she isn't going to at all.

Karlie, why did you leave without saying goodbye? Now you won't answer my calls. What did I do? I miss you already. Please call me. I need to hear you tell me it's all ok. I hope you are ok. I am miserable not being able to tell you goodbye or see you

before you left. I don't understand.

No reply. That is not like her. She usually has that phone connected to her hand at all times. Now I know something isn't right but what can I do? She chose to leave me without working it out. I guess I have to do the same. But this hurts more than I ever thought possible.

****

I keep watching my phone like it's going to magically ring and it be Aiden. He has to know by now that I left Colvin early. I bet he is very angry with me. Can I blame him? I took the chicken way out. I ran away like a scared little girl. But seeing that look on his face again would have killed me. I couldn't look at him anyway after last night!

I hear the Dukes of Hazzard theme song play on my phone and I know without looking that it's Aiden's ringtone. I can't talk to him. I hit ignore and send him to my voicemail and shut my phone off. No one can get a hold of me now. I just lay my head back against the head rest and close my eyes. I didn't sleep very well last night so I could use a little shut eye. If my mind will let me, that is.

Before I know it, I have drifted off and Mom is trying to wake me up once we make it to Tulsa and asks, "Want to go get an early lunch before going to the airport?"

"Sure." Is all I can get out. I really need to leave Oklahoma but I do have quite a bit of time to kill before my plane leaves. I could probably eat and I know my parents to would like the extra time with me too.

"AJ just called and said that Aiden came by the house to see you this morning but we were already gone. He is pretty upset you didn't say goodbye to him. What's going on Karlie?"

"I told him goodbye last night."

"He didn't see it that way. This isn't like you two. What happened last night?"

"Can we just not talk about Aiden anymore? I am leaving for LA in a couple of hours and I need to concentrate on school. UCLA is going to be hard and I am so excited to be going to LA."

"Karlie Mae, I know what you are doing. You are changing the subject. I will drop it for now." And with that we pull into the first restaurant and head inside. These next couple of hours are going to drag on. I want to be on the plane now and heading to my new life. My new life away from Colvin. And Aiden.

After we eat and start to head for the airport, I turn my phone on to text Savannah and let her know we were headed to the airport. I wanted to text Aiden, but I had to make myself hit Savannah instead. As my phone comes on I see that a text has been received. I open it up and see that it's from Aiden.

Karlie, why did you leave without saying goodbye? Now you won't answer my calls. What did I do? I miss you already. Please call me. I need to hear you tell me it's all ok. I hope you are ok. I am miserable not being able to tell you goodbye or see you before you left. I don't understand.

Oh boy. Tears are filling my eyes and I can do nothing but sit here in this seat and reread the words over and over not knowing what to say or if I even can say anything back. Why did I let things change between us last night? How stupid was I to think he could love me like I do him? And now I have lost my best friend too…

I just hit delete and send a quick text to Savannah.

Almost to airport. I am so excited!! Talk soon!

And after I hit send I turn the power back off on the phone and shove it into my purse, take a deep breath and exhale slowly. I just have to think positive and things will be alright. I can't think about Aiden and how he felt kissing me and touching me last night. Ahhhhhh!

"Well, here we are baby girl. I will get your bags and then you and Mom are ready. I can't believe I am sending my baby off to college. Doesn't seem real. I am very proud of you though, Karlie Mae. I pray you always know that. I love you."

Mom and I grab our bags and head for security. I am really going to LA!! I am beginning to get excited and nervous all in one. Thank goodness Mom is flying with me to LA and helping me get settled. I had hoped Aiden would come with me, but never had the nerve to ask if he would come. Sure glad I didn't now. This would be excruciating with him now after last night. Ok, no more thinking about last night or Aiden. Only LA and the future! LA. Future in LA. LA. LA. LA.

2

Eight years later....

Nearing the limits of Colvin I feel myself going back in time. I haven't been back here since I left for LA. I wouldn't be back now either if it weren't for my father just having a stroke. Mom needs help with his care and her baked goods store. I'm in between shoots now so I have a few weeks to spare before deciding what my next one will be. I just wish I were going to spend them anywhere but here in Colvin. Middle of Nowhere, Oklahoma. I'm really not looking forward to this. Thankfully Mom and Dad live on this side of town and I don't have to venture too far into the town limits.

Pulling up in front of the house I grew up in, I feel a pang of nausea come over me. The last time I pulled up here I was rushing away from someone after the most incredible encounter of my life. The most difficult encounter of my life. I shake it off and put my car in park. I flew into the Tulsa airport and rented a car to go the last 100 miles to Colvin knowing it would be easiest to have Mom stay with Dad and not coming to get me. But now, I wish I had driven the whole way from LA to give myself more time to prepare.

As I open my car door Mom comes running out with such a sweet look on her face that makes me feel a bit guilty. Maybe I should have come back before now. Instead of sending them tickets to see me wherever I was on my latest shoot, I should have come home.

"Baby you're home!!" screams Mom as she runs across the driveway.

"Hi Mom. How are you and how's Dad?" I ask fighting back the tears as she gives me the biggest hug I have ever gotten from her. She has been carrying the weight of Dad's illness on her own. I came as soon as Mom called me but I was in London on a shoot so it took me a couple of days to get here.

"He is having a tough day but will be so happy to see his baby girl."

We walk arm in arm inside the house and I swallow all the guilt and pain I feel about being back here again after all these years. Now isn't the time for that. There will be plenty of time for that later.

"Hi Dad! How are you feeling today?"

"Better now that you are here baby!" he says with his face lighting up when seeing me.

"I brought you a new postcard from London to add to your collection." I hand him the card knowing he has one from every place that I have been.

"This one's my favorite Karlie Mae. I always wanted to take your Mom there after we got married but thankfully we got to go and see you there last year." Dad says with pride shining in his eyes. "I hope you know how proud of you we are."

"Let me get my stuff settled into my room Dad then we will play some cards or something until bed." I say hugging him and carrying my stuff to my old room. Walking to my room for the first time since I left and I am shocked to see that it is exactly the same way I left it eight years ago.

****

After going to college in Tulsa, I was able to come back home with a new set of eyes and see things like a man would instead of the boy I used to be. I worked side by side with my Dad and Gene to learn everything that I didn't already know about running a ranch and making it a successful business venture. This land is in my blood and I am very proud to have a chunk of it for my future.

Today I got up and drove the fences that border my land from my parents' and I still have to pinch myself because I really do own 100 acres of the land that my ancestors have been on for generations. It makes my heart swell to know that I have been blessed with the success that I needed with my own cattle and horses to be able to purchase the exact land that I wanted seven years ago.

Walking back into my kitchen I see that my girlfriend Tracey has stopped by and must be making me some breakfast. She is a great girl and my sister's best friend. It took me a few years after Karlie left to get myself back out there and date but when Audrey told me I should ask Tracey out, it was a no brainer. She is beautiful, sweet, I have known her for years, and she was around. Not in LA. That was a little over three years ago, and here we are.

"Aiden, honey, do you think we will ever get married? We have been together for three years!" Tracey asks from across the kitchen.

"I don't know if I'm ready for that. I have explained that to you a hundred times. I love being with you, just not sure I want to get married yet." I say in the softest voice I can to cover the frustration I feel over this redundant conversation. I think she asks me twice a day. Every day.

"But you do love me, right?" she squeaks out with a pouty face that drives me insane.

"Yes Tracey, I love you." I say quickly then get up to go to the restroom. Where there is peace and quiet.

I do love her. I do. There is just something missing with her and I just wonder if it's me that's missing. Am I not putting my all into this relationship? What would keep me from committing completely to a beautiful and sweet girl like Tracey? I am almost 27 years old and I feel as if something is missing. I just don't know what it is.

I walk to my bedroom and out onto the deck that overlooks the south pasture and creek. The creek that Karlie and I went to all the time. The one we fished out of and where we made love. Well, I thought it was making love but she didn't think so. And now I remember that every time I look out my back windows.

Ah, I have to get past this. She has been gone for eight years and I have Tracey. I have this ranch and my family. I have everything any man could want out of life. But why aren't I content?

"I'm sorry I pressured you again Aiden, I just get carried away sometimes when I see what our life could be like." Tracey says as she comes up behind me wrapping her arms around my waist.

I put my arms on hers and sigh, "I know maybe it is time I start planning for the future. Our future."

I only wish that didn't taste so bad coming out of my mouth. My stomach didn't seem to enjoy it either.

"The AK Ranch is all I have ever wanted and now I have it. I also have you. Give me a little more time and I promise things will change. I do love you Tracey. We can go to town soon and look at rings ok?" I turn around and plant a quick kiss on her forehead and walk towards the door. I need to get out of here and figure out a way to start these changes we talked about, knowing they will be easier said than done.

The AK Ranch was supposed to be for Karlie and me. That's the reason it's called the AK Ranch. Aiden-Karlie.... Geez what did I do? I started the ranch a year after she left with confidence she would come back to me and tell me she loved me. Was I ever wrong. How am I going to marry Tracey and live on the AK Ranch with her?? How do I plan a future with her that includes children that I always wanted to have with Karlie? Karlie. Karlie. Karlie.

****

"KAB Photos will be back in business as soon as I get back from Oklahoma. Yes, I am thinking about where I want to take my next assignment Gerry, I will let you know. Thanks." I say to my friend and mentor from LA. Gerry was the one who took a chance on a girl from Oklahoma and let her spread her artistic wings with a $1,000 camera. What a whirlwind it has been since then. A whirlwind of celebrities, exotic locations, lots of money, new hotels every week, and of course new clients and opportunities coming from all directions. Everything I dreamed of growing up.

"KAB photos." Dad says from behind me. "Love the name baby. Does Aiden know?"

"No, I haven't spoken to him since I left Dad. I started it after college. I didn't know I wouldn't see him again when I named it. Think it's time to change it? You haven't told him either have you?"

"Aiden doesn't know dear even though he always asks me about you. Since he was a boy he has been your best friend. What happened before you left to end all that? I always thought you two would get married and give me grandchildren someday. I'm not going to be around forever you know."

"Nothing, I just had to go. You know how I felt about Colvin. Well, still kinda do Dad."

"I have worked for the 6AB Ranch for 40 years and have made a great life for our family. Didn't I? How could you hate it here that much?"

"I just wanted to take pictures Dad and be known around the world. I didn't want to be a nobody here like I always was." I say with too much emotion. I turn and walk away knowing I am too emotional to continue this conversation.

"Karlie wait, you have to talk about this. Is there anyone in LA?" He asks not sure if he wants to know the answer. "Didn't your mother say she met a man the last time she went to see you?"

"Jeremy is a great guy Dad and yes he has been talking about marriage but I told him I had to think about it and would answer him when I got back from here. It just doesn't feel right Dad. He is wonderful, I love him, but not sure I want to spend the rest of my life with him." I say wiping tears from my eyes.

"Aiden is what's wrong with you Karlie Mae. You love him still don't you?" Dad asks as he sits down out of breath.

"I haven't seen or talked to him in over eight years, Dad. How could I still love him?" I say feeling the tears stream down my cheeks knowing he is probably right.

"You need closure baby, but I can't tell you what to do. You have been here for almost a week and you haven't left this house. You go with me to the doctor appointments but that's it. You have to venture outside that front door and find yourself again. Make sure you know who you are and what it is that you want for your future before you leave to go back to LA."

"You're right; I do need to get out there. I'll go for a walk and maybe get some coffee at Sally's." I turn and kiss his cheek. "Thanks Dad, I love you."

3

Walking down the street I wonder what it was I hated about this town. It is so clean and everyone seems so nice as they wave and politely ask how I am. Maybe I was the problem back then. This is nice though. In LA no one looks at you and no one smiles. Here it seems so laid back and easy. I see kids playing in the town fountain so I take out my camera and snap a few pictures. I take a few of locals just doing what they do. A few of families loving and enjoying time with their children. Couples walking hand in hand radiating love. This is nothing like I remember this place being.

Before I know it I have taken at least a hundred snapshots. I haven't done that in forever. Just getting lost in my passion is what I used to love about photography. I haven't had the time to do that in the past few years. Maybe that is part of the problem too.

I walk in the door of Sally's Café and sit in what used to be my favorite spot in front of the window. After a few minutes Sally rushes over and gives me the strawberry and banana smoothie with a raisin bran muffin that I always used to get. She remembers. You would never find that in the big city. It warms my heart to know she remembered my favorites after all these years.

"Thanks Sally that's so sweet." I say smiling. "How have you been?" Looking at this lady makes me feel as if I never left. As if I was a teenager again.

"Things are great around here honey, it's been forever since you have been in here! We have all missed seeing your beautiful face. How has LA been treating you?" she asks full of energy and a huge smile.

"It has been great. My business is booming and I never know where I'll be next. Here for a little while to help Mom and Dad out since he's been so sick."

"I sure pray your Daddy gets better soon sweetie. Your mama sure has a wonderful store over there. That's where all my pastries and baked goods come from. I would hate for her to have to close down to care for him." She says quickly before running to the next customer.

I turn to look out the window just in time to see the one person I was praying I would not run into. The one person I didn't think I could handle seeing again. And I was right; I can't even though my heart has leapt into my throat. But I can't look away.

Aiden has filled out and gotten so much taller. He is tan and strong from working on his parent's ranch all these years. Wow. And that smile that melted my insides all these years and those arms that held me and touched me that one special night together. Wow have I ever missed him.

"Oh that's Tracey Wheeler with Aiden. Nice little gal. I think they'll be getting engaged soon. Don't they just look so in love?" Where did she come from?

"Yes, I suppose they do. How long have they been together?" Hearing the word engaged felt like a knife through my heart. I hope my face isn't giving me away.

"About three years, I think. We all used to think you two would be married by now but when you didn't come back we all had to move on right?"

They all had to move on? What does she mean by that? Aiden didn't want to marry me any more than he wanted to poke his eye out. He was ashamed of our night together. She must be mistaken. Must be. Has to be.

He sure is a sight though. I think as I turn back to the window. Wow. Jeremy doesn't hold a candle to Aiden. Wait? What did I just say? Oh brother I have to get out of here. I knew this was a bad idea. I should have stayed at Mom and Dad's. If I run now I can escape before they get any closer or see me.

I pay for my smoothie and muffin hurrying out of the café as fast as my feet would carry me which is straight into Aiden and his blonde bimbo. Just my luck.

"Oh, I'm so sorry I wasn't watching where I was-"

"Karlie Mae, is that you? What are you doing here?" Aiden asks with too much shock in his voice while holding onto my waist to steady me.

"I am helping Mom out with Dad for a little bit. How are you?" I ask trying to cover the cracking of my voice and pulling away composing myself. He is even more handsome up close. Those eyes of his that still melt my insides...

"We were looking at rings at the jeweler down the block. We are thinking of getting married. Aren't we baby?" Tracey says sweetly. If only she knew how badly I wanted to run away. How hard it is for me to keep these burning tears at bay.

"Yes we are thinking about it. Tracey, can you wait in the pickup while I catch up with Karlie for a minute?" He says kissing Tracey's forehead.

"I have to go anyway, nice to see you." I say hurrying off before Aiden could say anything or before the tears broke free.

That could not have gone any worse. He wants to marry her? That hurt. I wanted to be the one to marry Aiden my entire life. But he didn't want me. He wanted miss blonde bombshell. Not green eyes and brown haired me.

I start to run back to Mom and Dad's house. That was horrible. Tears are for sure flowing now.

"Baby girl, what is wrong?" Dad asks when I rush in the door crying.

"Oh Dad!" I say running to him and collapsing into his hug.

"By the state of you I can see you must have run into Aiden?" he guesses correctly rubbing my back to comfort me but I can't say a word. I know he will just let me cry it out.

****

"Was that Karlie Doone from your class?" Tracey asks when I get into the pickup shaking off the uneasiness of that encounter. I can't believe that just happened. She's back.

"Yes, that's her. I didn't know she was back. Haven't seen her since graduation." I say trying to cover my emotions. It feels like yesterday that she left. And didn't come back.

"What's she doing back here now?"

"Couldn't tell ya."

Seeing Karlie after all these years really sent my insides in a tailspin. She is so beautiful! Her brown hair is so shiny and her tan is gorgeous. LA must really work for her. Those green eyes sparkling like emeralds. She is the most gorgeous woman I have ever seen. I thought she was pretty before but now she is 100% woman and sexy!

But not my woman. She never has been my woman. Where had that come from? Tracey is sitting next to me in the pickup and I am thinking of another woman.

"You sure are quiet now. Are you upset about the rings?" Asks Tracey before we pull up to her apartment. "You have been distant since we left downtown."

"Sorry just have a lot going on at the ranch this afternoon. Took a bit more time than I anticipated in town." I say quickly dodging her question. "I will see you soon ok. Love you." I give her a quick kiss as I drop her off at her apartment before heading back to the ranch. My ranch. The AK Ranch. Not the AT Ranch. What I am I supposed to do now? I have 500 head of cattle with the AK brand on them. Not that easy to change. Oh brother....

4

"Aiden, what's up?"

"Hey man. Just came by to see how things were going."

"Very good. We have been very busy. I know you didn't come by to talk flowers. What's up?"

"Oh nothing important. Just thought I would swing by and see my brother, what's wrong with that?"

"What's wrong is that your brother knows this has nothing to do with him and most likely to do with a certain Miss Doone that is back in town. Am I right?"

"You're good. Yes it has to do with Karlie."

"Have you seen her or talked to her?"

"I literally ran into her outside of Sally's the other day but we didn't say much. She rushed off too quick."

"How does she look? I know you had the hots for her from middle school to high school. Heck you probably still do!" He laughs and punches me in the arm.

"Ha ha brother very funny. I can't deny that she is more gorgeous now than she ever was before. Or at least that I can remember. I was stunned when this lady ran into me on the sidewalk and when she looked up it was those green eyes that used to haunt me even after she left."

"That was poetic man. You should write a book or something. Why don't you go tell her that and not me? Look her in those haunting eyes and profess your undying love." He is getting way too much enjoyment out of this.

"You are no help Austin. I came here for some brotherly advice and all you can do it make fun of me."

"Aww are you gonna cry? Here let me get you a tissue to wipe your tears."

"Bite me. I'm outta here." I walk to my pickup and scowl Austin's way as he stands in front of the nursery doors laughing. What a jerk. I should have known he wasn't the one to go to about this.

"Dude I was just kidding. Come back in here and I promise not to make fun."

"Yea right. You were enjoying that too much. I'm all freaking out over here and you just laugh."

"Why are you freaking out? You have Tracey. Or does that old flame still burn for Karlie?"

"I didn't think I still had feelings for Karlie after what happened when she left, that was so long ago. But when I saw her face it took my breath away and I felt like someone punched me in the gut. My head has been spinning ever since. What am I supposed to do now?"

"Talk to her you dope. She may not even remember your friendship. She has been gone a long time and living the high life. Or at least that's what I have heard you and Gene talking about over the years."

"Yea, you're right. I doubt she even cares about me. She is the one that left and never looked back. I just can't get that encounter out of my head. She ran away like she was upset but that can't be right."

"You seriously need to talk to her. Don't just lay it all out there, just make small talk and see what happens. Your girlfriend might not like you talking to the woman you pined for all these years though."

"Tracey. What do I do about her? It sounds selfish and all but if Karlie doesn't feel the same for me, I don't want to lose Tracey too."

"So you aren't the perfect gentleman that everyone thinks you are. You're human. You are allowed to have mixed feelings after seeing the once love of your life Aiden.

You were really hurt when she left. Left things unfinished. Maybe this is the closure you will need."

"Thanks man. I gotta go do chores. Talk soon."

"Bye Romeo. Let me know what Juliet 1 or Juliet 2 says." He laughs again but this time I don't turn back.

I start my pickup and drive away not feeling any better than I did before coming here. What do I do now? I could always call her parents' house and hope she answers. Or maybe I shouldn't in case her mom or dad answers. How do I explain why I am calling? We used to be friends it would be ok to call now right?

Telling myself it's ok to call an old friend that's in town for a bit, I dial the Doone family phone number and wait anxiously to hear Karlie's voice on the other end. No answer. They must be outside. Or maybe Gene had another appointment. I will call later. Or not. I shouldn't be bothering them; she is home to help with Gene's care not to see me. I need to get over all of this before I mess it up with Tracey.

****

A few days after seeing Aiden I decide to pull myself away from the house and the pain while Mom takes Dad to another doctor appointment and to do what I love to do most. Take pictures. And just like last time, I get lost in my work and the joy I find in catching life with a camera lens.

I find a young mother-to-be-soon sitting on a bench in the park watching the other little kids play on the slide. She looks so happy and excited to become a mother. I feel a pang of jealousy as I watch her rub her swollen stomach. I am beginning to think I will never become a mother myself. Will I ever have a baby of my own? Will I ever have a husband that takes care of me when I am so pregnant?

After a few hours I open the front door to the house and see Mom crying and talking to someone on the phone. They must have just gotten back from his doctor appointment. She isn't looking good so that means Dad isn't doing well.

"Mom, what's wrong. Where is Dad? What's going on?" I cry out starting to panic as I race towards her.

"Honey, your Dad is in the hospital. He isn't doing well. I just came home to get his medicines and then going back. Do you want to follow me there?" she says crying and shaking.

"Mom, I was gone a couple of hours. How did this happen so fast? Why didn't you call me?" I ask aloud, desperate to know.

"He started having trouble breathing in the waiting room of the doctor's office and they rushed him to the ER and he was put in the hospital. He is in ICU and not looking well baby. They say he is possibly having another stroke. I did try you but your phone was off. I tried several times and left numerous messages."

"Let's go Mom. I need to see Dad. I'll drive you." On the way to the car I notice that my phone was off. I never turn it off. I'm really not myself am I? After seeing Aiden with Blondie and now my Dad is fighting for his life how could I be?

****

"Aiden, it's Mom. I just got a call from Ella Mae. They have admitted Gene into the hospital and they think he is having another stroke. Your Dad and I are headed over there now just wanted you to know." Mom says quietly on the other end of the phone.

"Oh wow. Thanks Mom, give them my love. Keep me posted." I say in shock. What do I do now? Do I go to the hospital knowing that Karlie will be there or just stay away? Let my parents be there?

I dial my sister's number. "Audrey, what do I do about Tracey? I am not sure we want the same things anymore." I ask. "She is pressuring me to propose but I am not sure that's what I want."

"Well, hello brother. Just be honest with her. She is a great person and deserves honesty. Is it Karlie or what?"

"What do you mean, Karlie? I just saw her yesterday for the first time in eight years. How could that be my issue with Tracey?" I ask too quickly. "This has nothing to do with Karlie."

"We all know you have loved Karlie your whole life. I thought Tracey was a good person to show you another side of life. Was I maybe wrong about that?"

"And I do love Tracey. I just need to get some things straight in my head. She is my future right?" I ask trying to sound convincing.

"Love you brother." And she hangs up leaving me to my own thoughts. Thoughts of Karlie and her family. Audrey wasn't any help. Thanks a lot sis.

****

I find myself entering the hospital with terrible fear as I follow Mom to Dad's room. All of my emotions are on high. How can this be happening? I was only gone a few hours and in those few hours our lives have been turned upside down. Walking into Dad's room, I clearly see that he is not doing well at all. He is hooked up to every machine possible and isn't even breathing on his own. This is so scary.

I take a break from my own emotions to see Mom sitting next to Dad and she looks as pale as he is. She is holding his hand and stroking it lightly with a very frightened look on her face. She is touching him as if he were fragile while I remember him being so strong and full of life. I walk to her and stand behind her putting my hands on her shoulders. As I do I feel her body quiver as she cries.

"What will we do without him Karlie? He can't leave me yet." She says through sobs and tears. "This just can't be happening."

"Mom, we just have to pray that he will pull through this. We know how tough he is." I lean down and hug her from behind. I'm not sure who I am trying to convince, her or me. I wish Jonathan were here. My brother is in Iraq and hasn't been able to come home since last Christmas. He would know what to say and do to help.

I decide I have to call him but don't want to say the words. I walk outside the room and pull my cell out of my pocket. I dial the number given for emergency contact with him; I realize that I have to be the one to break the news to him. I can't let Mom do it. It has to be me.

I leave a message for them to relay to him as soon as possible. Of course they can't guarantee when that will be. I just pray it's soon.

Hanging up and putting my phone back in my pocket and I just can't find the strength to go back in the room. I then hear someone calling my name from down the hall. Turning my head I can see it's Amelia and AJ Blake which are Aiden's parents. They must have just gotten off the elevators. By the looks on their faces they are as upset as we are.

Amelia opens her arms and wraps me in one of the hugs that melt your worries away. Stepping into her embrace feels right and for the most part comforting. Even if I am not with Aiden she will always mean the world to me.

"What do we know honey?" Asks AJ from behind us.

I untangle myself from Amelia's hug and look at AJ. I can't seem to get a word out so he just pulls me into an embrace also. And as I relax against his strong chest I feel the tears begin to surface. Before I know it I am sobbing uncontrollably.

"It's okay, sweetheart. Let it out. We are all so scared for your father."

I don't realize it at first but Amelia has gone into Dad's room. She will be a great comfort to Mom. AJ and I head in to see them standing on each side of Dad's bed. They seem to be saying a prayer for him and when they finish Mom seems a little bit more in control.

"Aiden and the rest of the ranch send their love your way." Amelia says as she helps Mom sit back down next to Dad's bed. She looks at me and smiles.

"Thank you guys for coming. It means the world to all of us." Mom says between sobs and squeezes Dad's hand.

"If you don't mind I would like to be alone with Gene for a little while."

"Sure Mom. Call me if you need anything or if there are any changes. I'll be back with dinner. Love you." I say and kiss her forehead. It just breaks my heart more to see her so upset.

Amelia, AJ and I walk quietly to the elevator and once outside the hospital I stop and take a deep breath. This is going to be the most horrific night of my life. Dad could very well never wake up. Amelia and AJ both grab one of my hands and walk me to my car.

As I climb in behind the wheel, it hits me that I am going home to an empty house. My parents' empty house. The weight of the situation hits. What will we do if Dad doesn't pull through? What will Mom do without the love of her life? Now tears are flowing from my eyes and I barely remember driving home.

Opening the front door I start to feel defeated and exhausted. This house may never be the same. I can see

Dad everywhere. I should have come home more often. All of this time away from them was wasted on my career and fears of being a nobody. And now I am standing here alone. Completely alone.

I pull my cell phone out of my pocket again and dial Jeremy's number. Voice mail. Imagine that. I really could use strong arms to hold me right now. Aiden comes to mind but he's holding Tracey right now. Knowing that things are beyond my control, I can't help but throw myself on my bed and cry uncontrollably like I used to when I was a child.

****

"Aiden it's really bad. They are not sure Gene will make it. He had a massive stroke this time." Mom says as she walks into the barn. "You need to go see him and Ella Mae before it's too late. And Karlie."

"Mom are you sure that's appropriate? I'm with Tracey and not a part of their family." I say clearly being torn in two by this decision.

"Aiden my son, you have known the Doone's almost your entire life. Regardless how your relationship with Karlie has been, you two were inseparable until she left for LA. You are like Gene and Ella Mae's other son. It would be a comfort to her to know you came by. And Karlie isn't there right now. She told her Mom she would come back with dinner." Mom says standing in front of the stall I am in to ensure that she has my full attention.

"It breaks my heart to know there isn't anything I can do for Karlie, Mom. What do I say to her? But I will go as soon as I'm done in here. Thanks for letting me know." I say genuinely grateful for such a wonderful mother.

"I will talk to you later, son. I love you." And with that she walks out of the barn. Leaving me alone to ponder my thoughts. This all seems so unreal.

Now I need to go see Gene. I wouldn't be able to live with myself if he passed away without seeing him at least one more time. Hopefully I can be in and out of there before Karlie gets back.

****

"Aiden, thank you so much for coming. Gene will be so happy to know you are here. He always has thought of you as another son." Ella Mae says as she stands and hugs me when I enter Gene's room. "We always hoped that you and Karlie Mae would fall in love, get married, and give us lots of grandkids."

"You two mean the world to me too. I'm sorry she and I weren't able to do that for you." I say tying to be comforting and not make her feel worse. She has no idea how much I wanted all of that too.

I sit with her for a few minutes and we reminisce about growing up on the 6AB. Some of her memories I had forgotten. They all seem to involve Karlie though.

"Would you mind sitting with Gene for a few minutes while I go talk to the doctor? I don't want to leave him alone."

"Of course not, go ahead. Anything you need. For as long as you need." I say helping her to the door. I can't help but see the fragile state that she is in and the amount of worry that is resting on her. My heart just breaks for Ella Mae.

After shutting the door, I walk over to Gene's bedside and grab his hand. It is so hard to see such a strong man be so still and look so fragile. This is the exact opposite of the man I have known my whole life.

"I'm not sure if you can hear me or not, but I wanted to tell you that I am so sorry this has happened. You need to come back to your wife and kids. They need you now more than ever. Karlie will be there for Ella Mae, but I am afraid no one will be there for Karlie. It's going to kill her to lose you and we both know she is too stubborn to ask for help. I know you always aimed to get us together but she just didn't feel the same as I did. As I do? I'm not really sure anymore. Just please come back to us Gene." Saying what I needed to say brings tears to my own eyes. I put my head down on the bed and recite a prayer. It just so happens to be the one that

Gene taught me as a child. The one that we would say before every cow or horse passed away.

****

Opening the door to Dad's room I am surprised to see Aiden there with his head down on Dad's bed. He looks so handsome and sad all in one. It makes my heart jerk but I wonder what he is doing here.

"Aiden? What are you doing here? Where is my mother?"

"Oh! Hi, Karlie. I just came to check on your Mom and Dad and she asked me to sit with him while she talked to his doctor." Aiden says while standing up quickly and wiping tears away. "I'll go now that you are here."

As I see him heading towards the door I feel as if another part of me is being torn out. Seeing this man shed tears for my father tugs at my heart.

"Please stay Aiden." I say and smile as best I can at him. "There is another chair over there."

"Are you sure Karlie?" he asks making sure I know what I am doing. "I can go if you want to be alone."

"I don't really want to be alone right now." We both know that there won't be any speaking, just the comfort of him being here with me helps to ease a bit of the pain inside.

After a few minutes of us sitting in the quiet, Mom walks back in the door. Aiden stands up and says he has to go. He gives Mom a hug and I walk into his arms after. It seems like instinct to do such a thing with him.

"Call if you need anything." He says and quickly rushes off. As if touching me was repulsive.

I will never understand that man. He acted excited to see me downtown but now he couldn't get away from me fast enough. He didn't have to be that rude!

"Oh Karlie, I didn't expect to see you back here this soon. Why did Aiden leave so quickly?" Mom asks as she heads to Dad's bedside again.

"I'm not sure what his deal was, Mom. So, what did the doctor say? And the attorney was here? Why?"

"No changes. They say there isn't anything more they can do for him Karlie. They don't think he will make it another day." Mom says starting to cry whole heartedly again.

"Oh Mom! I'm so sorry this is happening to you! It isn't fair. This can't be happening! I just talked to him this morning before I left for my walk. How can he not be coming out of this?" I say losing my control and crying too.

****

"Karlie, you let us know if you need anything. Day or night. You two are not alone." Mom says as she hangs up the phone. I can see by her expression and posture that something is wrong.

"What is it Mom?" I ask alarmed by the words I heard and the tears she was shedding.

"Gene isn't going to get any better. There is nothing the doctors can do. They don't think he will make it another day." Mom says clearly shaken up by this news. "I need to go find your father and tell him the terrible news."

I give my Mom a big hug and hope it conveys my feelings for her. I just stand here in the kitchen stunned by the news about Gene. This can't be happening.

"Baby, are you ready to leave for Tulsa? It's the romantic weekend we have been planning." I hear Tracey say as she comes up behind me into the kitchen too. "What's wrong?"

"Gene Doone is being taken off of life support in the morning." I say feeling as if I am talking to a stranger about this.

"He was a good foreman here wasn't he? Sad to know you'll have to replace him yes, but why are you ready to fall apart over it?" Tracey asks clearly unsure of the depth of this situation. "I know you were friends with his daughter growing up but were you close to him also?"

"Yes, Tracey. I am. Was. Whatever. He has been the foreman here for longer than I have been alive. He's going to be greatly missed. Such a good man." I say getting annoyed. "I've got to go. Cancel our weekend or take Audrey with you since it's all paid for. I just can't leave right now."

I see her stick her bottom lip out to pout but thinks better of it when I turn to look at her still standing in my Mom's kitchen.

"I need to be here if Kar- Ella Mae or anyone needs me." And with that I walk out of the house and to my pickup. I have to drive somewhere, anywhere to be alone. Alone to think. Alone to grieve.

****

"Jeremy, it's me. I know you are busy but I really need you right now. Dad had a stroke and won't make it. I really need you. Please call me back or get on a plane and come here in person. I need you. Bye." That has to be the 100th voicemail I have left that man.

Mom stayed at the hospital with Dad so I'm here in this house alone. I just can't believe he will never be back in it. He will be gone soon. We have a funeral to plan now. Thankfully Mom and Dad already did most of the arrangements ahead of time. I used to think that was very odd but now I have to say I understand why. Mom and I couldn't make those decisions right now. As I sigh I decide that a glass of wine and a hot bath would be great and might help ease some of this pain.

Finding my iPod and ear buds, I put them in and push play on my favorite playlist. I undress and sink slowly into the hot sudsy bathwater. Losing myself in the music, wine and emotions. Letting the outside world slip away even if it is only for a short time.

5

I find myself in front of Karlie's parents' house. There is an unfamiliar car in the driveway that must be her rental. It just breaks my heart to know she is in there alone and grieving. I want so badly to wrap her in my arms and kiss her hurt away.

Before I know it, I am walking up to the front door and knocking. No answer. I knock again. This is strange she isn't answering when all the lights are on inside. I hope she is ok. I try the knob and it turns. Not locked. She hasn't learned a thing from living in the big city all these years. I call out her name but she still doesn't answer. Knowing where her room is I walk towards it seeing the light on inside. But before I can get there, I am distracted by the bathroom door being open an inch and seeing Karlie in the bathtub full of bubbles, earphones in, and wine in hand. She is singing to herself and relaxing. What I wouldn't give to be in there sitting behind her with my arms around her and kissing her neck. Telling her how much I love her, telling her everything will be ok.

I hear water splash around and am drawn out of my daydream. She is starting to get out so I had better get out of here before she sees me. I don't want to upset her anymore. I am not really sure how she would react seeing me here tonight. Especially knowing she isn't wearing anything but bubbles.

As I walk back down the hallway towards the front door I can't help but look around and memories start to flood me as I do. I can see Ella Mae sitting Karlie on the counter in the kitchen cleaning up her scraped knees after we crashed our bikes in 5th grade. Or when we went to Homecoming together that first year of high school. Karlie looked so pretty in her yellow knee length dress and hair all curled up.

I think I knew at that Moment she was the one for me. I can even remember prom that last year before Karlie left me. We were so nervous because we both knew it was the last prom we would have. And we both knew she would be leaving in a couple of months for LA. I even spent so many Moments in this house after she left. This place will never be the same without Gene. Ella Mae and Karlie won't either. Letting myself out the front door, I make sure and turn off all the lights. I also turn the lock on the door knob because I know that Karlie won't think to check that.

Climbing into my pickup I sit and stare at the bedroom light that's on which I know is Karlie's. I can see shadows on the window and see that she is getting dressed. I imagine that she is wearing one of those long t-shirts of her Dad's that she loved to wear. How do I leave her here alone?

After a few minutes I see her bedroom light go dark. I picture her lying in her bed crying and alone. That just breaks my heart. I will just sit out here until she surely has to be asleep.

****

That bath felt wonderful or maybe it was all the wine. Or maybe both. Toweling off and dressing in one of Dad's t-shirts I continue to think of what lies ahead of us.

When I am all ready for bed I walk into the kitchen and living rooms to turn off the lights. They are already off. That's strange; I thought I left them on. Walking back into my bedroom and shutting off the light, I can't help but let my mind wander to Aiden. How did he take the news about Dad? Maybe I should call him. Why am I thinking about him? When aren't I?

As I lay here in the dark I can't help but let the memories flood in. Dad, Jonathan, and of course Aiden is a part of all of them. Most of them are at the creek or 6AB. I will no longer have ties to them after tomorrow. I will no longer have my father. I wish Aiden were here to hold me like he always did when we were kids. He always knew how to make me feel better no matter what it was I was upset about. What I wouldn't do to be in his arms right now.

But instead, he is holding her. Loving her. Going to marry her. Not me. Not me.

****

Knock knock. Knock knock.

I awake with a jump. I feel disoriented and confused. My whole body hurts and I don't understand where I am. I sit up and realize Austin is knocking on my pickup window. I am still parked in front of Karlie's. It's still so dark outside. I must not have been asleep very long.

"What's up Austin?" I say trying to sound natural as I roll the window down. Like it's not strange that I am sleeping in my pickup in front of Karlie's house.

"What are you doing man? Mom is frantic because you didn't come home or go to your house. And here I find you asleep in your pickup in front of the Doone's house." Austin says clearly getting too much enjoyment out of this situation.

"I just came to check on Ella Mae and Karlie and must have fallen asleep. What time is it anyway?"

"Aiden, it's four in the morning and Ella Mae stayed at the hospital with Gene. How long have you been here? Did you go in and see Karlie at all?"

"I came by right after dark. I was kinda tired but I didn't expect to stay long or fall asleep. You can go home now. I am. Thanks brother for looking for me. Tell Mom I am fine but not where I was, ok?"

"10-4. Be safe. Couple crazy days ahead."

I roll up my window and start my pickup. I can't help but take one more look towards Karlie's window. Still dark. Good, she will need the rest. Putting the pickup in drive and pressing on the accelerator just feels wrong. But I know it's all I can do. She isn't my girl. Not my responsibility. Not that she would allow me to be around if I tried.

Driving towards the ranch I notice that I have a few missed calls on my cell. Most of them my mother of course but one of them from Tracey. What would she think if she knew where I have been? I have got to get Karlie out of my head. This isn't fair to Tracey at all. But, how do I do that?

6

"Aiden, Gene is nearing the end. We will meet you at the hospital in a while. Karlie hasn't made it to the hospital yet, but Ella Mae said she should be there anytime. Love you son." I barely hear Mom say on the phone before hanging up.

Wow, this is it. He is going to die. I need to find Karlie. She is going to be a mess.

"Aiden, where are you?" I hear Tracey call out from the hallway right after I get off the phone.

"I'm in my bedroom getting ready to go to the hospital. Meeting my parents there." I say full of sadness and finish pulling on my boots. "What are you doing here? I thought you and Audrey left last night?"

"We changed it to this morning. I actually came to tell you good-bye. I had a certain good-bye in mind but I see from your mood that won't be happening." She says and sits next to me on the bed with a pout once again.

"No, sorry. I have to get going. You go and have fun with my sister. I'll see you when you get back."

"I was hoping after I get back that we could start moving my stuff onto the ranch." She says almost bashfully.

Here we go again. It never stops. "Tracey, I can't think about that right now. We will discuss it after your trip, yes. But no promises. You know how I feel."

"You promise?" she squeals and jumps up. "Oh Aiden, I love you!"

"Bye, Tracey. Be safe. Love you." That is getting harder and harder to say with a straight face to her. I have got to figure out what to do when it comes to her and our relationship.

But first I have to find Karlie. She is going to be a mess. She will be trying to be strong for Ella Mae and not let anyone be there for her. I will take my chance any way I can get it.

****

Today is going to be the toughest day of my life. Mom's too. I can't even begin to know how she is getting through all of this. Driving to the hospital after the worst night's sleep I feel like I'm moving in slow motion and in a thick fog. I don't really remember getting dressed or even driving across town to the hospital. I just can't seem to move my legs to get out of this car. How is someone supposed to do this? Maybe I should have stayed here last night with Mom. No, she said she needed the last night alone with Dad. But now I have to walk in there and say good-bye to the best father in the world. Good-bye. How do I do that?

Unable to hold my head up any longer, I rest it against the steering wheel knowing that I am merely stalling the inevitable. I feel the emotion overtaking me again and let go. I can be stronger for Mom if I get this all out now. Right? So here I sit slumped over in my rental car sobbing like a child.

Tap Tap

I barely hear the taps on the window over my sobbing. But as I do I look into the most gorgeous and kind eyes I have ever seen. Aiden. I frantically wipe the tears off my face and roll the window down.

"What are you doing here?" I ask still wiping tears and attempting to pull myself together. I must look like a disaster.

"Karlie, can I sit with you for a bit?" he asks and gestures towards the passenger seat. "Just for a minute?"

I just shake my head and unlock the doors. I wonder what he is doing here and why he wants to sit in my car with me. He must know I am a mess. He has to know it's not going to be easy for me. I suddenly realize how thankful I am that he is here as he slides into the seat next to me and just looks at me with that Aiden look on his face.

"Karlie, I can't even imagine how hard this is for you. I am so sorry." And with that he takes my hand and pulls me towards him and wraps his arms around me. As he does I just let go completely of all the emotion that has been eating away under the surface. I know that with Aiden I don't have to hide anything. He can simply look at me and know what I need.

"Just let it out. You don't have to be strong all the time. No one will see you now." He says and tightens his hug and kisses the top of my head. Oh how good this feels. I don't know what I would have done if he hadn't have come here today.

After a few minutes, I pull myself away and wipe the tears away taking big breaths and ask, "What are you doing here anyway?"

"Truth? I knew you would be upset and I wanted to be here in case you needed someone to lean on Karlie." Flashing me the smile that I have loved since I was five, it seemed to right a little bit of the world that was so far upside down.

"Aiden, I can't tell you how much I appreciate that. I don't know how to walk in there. How do I do that?" I ask and start to cry again. As I do I can feel his arms wrapping around me again.

"You just have to take it one step at a time. I will go with you if you want. I am here for you for anything." I know he means every word.

"I can't expect that of you, Aiden. You have your own life and a girlfriend that I am sure doesn't approve. Does she even know where you are?" I say trying to convince myself that I don't need his presence. Except I know that I might actually be able to get through this if he were by my side.

"She isn't the issue right now. You have to walk in there and say good-bye to your father; you need to focus on that. I am here for you, Karlie, regardless of whether you want me there today or not." He says opening his door and walks around the car to open mine.

I take one last deep breath and let it out slowly. Feeling so much better inside, I look up at Aiden as he opens my door and extends his hand to me. I put my hand in his knowing I honestly couldn't do this without him. I will worry about the consequences later.

"Remember, I'm here for you, Karlie. No matter what." And with that we walk towards the doors to the hospital with him holding my hand tight.

As we enter the ICU portion we can see the attorney, doctors and Reverend Lowell. They all have that pity look on their faces. That is the worst. The look of so much pity makes my stomach turn and my hands start to shake.

Aiden, knowing what I was thinking again, put his arm around my waist and pulls me close beside him. That seems like the most natural thing to have done to me at this painful time. I start to feel like I am actually strong enough to do this. All because of Aiden.

I walk into Dad's room and see that Mom has his hand in hers and she is praying. She actually looks at peace. How can that be? She is his wife and they are the love of each other's lives. How can I be such a mess and she isn't?

"Hi baby. How are you?" she asks walking over to give me a quick hug and kiss on my cheek. She does the same with Aiden. "Aiden, thank you so much for being here for Karlie and me."

"Don't mention it. I wouldn't want to be anywhere else." He says and smiles while wrapping his arm back around my waist.

She smiles and winks at me. "Karlie, do you want a few minutes alone with your Daddy?"

"Yes, please." I say and walk towards Dad feeling all the emotion and pain once again. But I feel arms wrap around me from behind as I start to get overwhelmed. Aiden has come up behind me and kisses the top of my head assuring me that he is here and that I can do this. "I'm ok, I need to do this. Thank you."

He and Mom walk out of the room leaving me alone with my father for the last time. I sit down on his bedside and take his pale hand in mine.

"Daddy, I don't know how to say good-bye to you. I wish things were so much different. Mom is being so strong and I worry that I can't do this or be strong for her. Well, maybe she doesn't need me to be strong, but I feel like I do. You were always that strength in our family. With you not here, someone has to. We can't get ahold of Jonathan either. He isn't going to be able to say good-bye Dad. I love you so much. I hope you know that. I am so sorry for not coming home these past eight years. I was so selfish. I'm going to miss you so much. How do I leave Mom now and go back to LA? Should I just move KAB here and work from Colvin? Dad you know how much that scares me but I feel like maybe that is what I am supposed to do. You were my biggest fan and I will continue to make you proud Dad. I promise. I love you Dad. Always will. Good-bye Daddy." I say a short prayer and feel my heart start to feel a bit lighter. Walking out of the room and seeing Aiden standing in the hallway with his arms around my mother makes me realize that life is so different. He is the other reason I should relocate to Colvin. Aiden is still a part of me. How have I done this without him so long? But then I also realize that he isn't mine. He is Tracey's. With that realization, my heart sinks but Mom is walking towards me and I know this is not the time.

****

What was that about? Why did Karlie change her demeanor towards me that quickly? I told her I was here for her no matter what. But she just dismissed me like I was nobody to her. Once again nobody to her.

I shake my head and walk to the elevators just in time to see my parents, siblings and Tracey getting off of one. They are looking just as glum as I feel.

"He's gone. I'm going back to the ranch, have things to take care of." Not even trying to hide the emotion in my voice. I get into an elevator and push the button I need and look to see Tracey trying to follow. I lift up my hand as a sign to stop her and shake my head. Thankfully she got the hint and Audrey took ahold of her arm to stop her too. I just can't deal with her and our issues right now. What is she even doing here with my family? I didn't tell her I was coming here.

You ok bro? Need company or alone time?

Text from Austin. I should have known they would let me go but he would be the one to try to help.

Alone time.

I wouldn't be much company and I want to sort out things with no one else there to make me talk about it.

While driving back to the ranch, I realize that the only place I feel like going to is the creek. I don't know what makes me want to go there after Karlie dismissed me so quickly, but that's where I feel closest to her. And now the only place to talk to Gene. Will she ever come back here to the creek now?

7

Dad's funeral is today. Mom and I have tried to get ahold of Jonathan with no luck and haven't heard back from him either. We don't even know if he has even about Dad. Knows that Dad is gone.

Helping Mom into the car is difficult. She is exhausted and beyond devastated. We both are but I know it's up to me to be strong for her. She has been strong for me my whole life and now it's time to return the favor. The funeral home limo came for us so that neither of us had to drive today. Not sure if that's the rule or if someone arranged it for u but I am just so thankful for not having to drive a car myself.

Pulling up to the funeral home I feel like I am in a movie. Or a dream. Seeing someone else go through this. Aiden and his brother Austin are there to open our doors for us. Austin on my side and Aiden on Mom's. It's a good thing he has a tight grip on me because I feel like I could pass out. The world is spinning and I can't get my footing.

****

Today is the day Karlie and Ella Mae have to say goodbye to Gene. We all have to say our goodbyes. It still doesn't seem real. We stand in front of the funeral home watching the limo pull up that is carrying Karlie and her mother. I take a deep breath and walk to the right side of the car hoping Karlie is on this side. Wrong, it's Ella Mae. Opening her door I peer in the car and see how pale both women are. They look like porcelain dolls that could easily be broken if handled too rough. I stretch my arm out for Ella Mae to grab onto and help her lift out of the car's backseat. I turn slightly to see if Austin is getting Karlie out ok. I have a slight case of jealousy because my brother gets to touch her and I don't. Even just a light touch of her hand on my arm for stability would mean the world to me. It would be more than I could hope for. But, I need to concentrate on keeping Ella Mae safe and getting her to the front of the service area.

I open the front door for Ella Mae and my own Mom and Dad rush over to us and relieve me of my duty. As I let them have Ella Mae's arm, I turn to see that Austin and Karlie are having trouble. She seems to be staggering as if she were tipsy. I run to her side just in time to catch her by the waist as she passes out.

"Karlie! Are you okay? Can you hear me? Karlie?" I exclaim with desperation filling my voice as I lower her to the ground. "Please Karlie, answer me. Karlie?"

I cradle her head in my lap and continue to rub her cheek and talk to her. She is still breathing so she must have just passed out. If she doesn't wake up in a few seconds I am going to call for an ambulance. I know she will be mad, but oh well if that's what I have to do to keep her safe.

"Karlie are you ok?" I can feel her breath on my cheek as I listen to make sure she is indeed still with us.

****

"Karlie, are you ok?" I hear Aiden asking me. He sounds like we are in a tunnel and far away from each other. What is going on? I open my eyes to realize I am in his arms lying on the ground in front of the funeral home. I must have actually passed out. Thankfully no one is around to witness my embarrassing situation. No one but Aiden.

"What happened? Where is everyone?" I ask trying to stand up on my own and get out of his arms but I am still a little woozy.

"Austin was helping you walk to the door and you started to pass out. He caught you and I ushered your Mom inside and ran back to help you. I was so worried about you

"I'm fine, thank you. And thanks for sparing Mom more worry. Can we go inside now? Tracey is probably worried. And I want to get this over with." I say walking away as fast as I can hoping to leave him a distance back.

"She's in Tulsa with Audrey. I'm here for as long as you need me. Your Mom too" He says rushing to catch up to my side and opens the door for me.

"Let's get this over with, please." I walk towards Mom and pray I am able to hold it all together a little bit longer. I can't help but look over at Aiden sitting there with his family. Why wouldn't she be here with him? Very strange. But then again, Jeremy isn't here either.

I pull myself out of my fog and try to concentrate on the words Reverend Lowell is saying about my Dad. The picture of him up there beside the casket shows him smiling with a horse. I know that picture well. It's a horse from the 6AB and Aiden and I are on the back of it. Of course we have been cropped out of it but I know. I wonder if Aiden knows too.

****

I wonder if Karlie recognizes that photo they used of her Dad. That's the day her Dad took us riding out onto the far north side of the ranch with him. She and I rode on one horse and Gene on another. That was a great day even though we both ended up sunburned to a crisp. Gene had told us to take hats with us but we didn't think we needed them. Karlie thought they were too boyish for a girl to wear and I didn't want to do anything she didn't want to do of course. I was hooked even at the age of eight.

As I hear everyone's kind words they are saying about Gene I can't help but keep a close eye on Karlie. She really scared me earlier when she passed out. I wonder when the last time was that she ate or slept.

****

The last words have been spoken and we are ready for the ride to the cemetery. This all still doesn't feel real. Walking out of the funeral home I see that our guests have all assembled into a group around our limo doors. Burial will be private so no one else will go with us from here. I see Aiden and Austin standing on the farthest side of the limo. They are clearly deep in conversation and I wonder to myself what they could be discussing.

Amelia and AJ are the first ones to come to Mom and me to offer their condolences. I melt into AJ's arms and feel lost. I once again feel as if I am watching a movie and not my life. They are saying something but I honestly don't hear them. I can only see Aiden in this haze and long to be comforted by him.

Once he finally comes over to us I am close to the edge and ready to fall apart. I must have it all written on my face because he comes directly to me and wraps me tightly into his arms. As he does I lose all control I had and sob into his chest. He holds me tight and kisses the top of my head. My heart is so full of hurt but I can still see that this is the man that I love more than life. I probably will always love him. I just can't have him.

I try to pull away but Aiden won't let me. He whispers no and turns us away from the crowd. We walk around the side of the building where no one will be able to see or hear me crying. He backs me up to the wall and puts distance between us so that he can look into my eyes. I can see so much hurt and pain in his eyes too and I sink back into his embrace.

"I am here Karlie, just remember that. You don't have to do this alone." He kisses my forehead one more time and walks us back to the limo and opens a door for me. As I climb in I turn to look at him one more time knowing it might be the last time.

"Thank you Aiden. For everything." I sit down on the limo seat and he shuts the door. Shuts out the world. Shuts me into this dark and dreary world I now live in.

Mom gets into the car next to me. She has stopped crying and looks almost at peace. How can she be so strong? She grabs my hand and we head to the cemetery to bury my father, her husband.

****

It kills me to know that I have to let Karlie go alone with her mother to the burial. After her fainting spell I really worry that she will do it again. Ella Mae isn't strong enough to catch her or help. I think I will just follow behind in my pickup but stay behind so they don't see me unless I am needed. Austin tried talking me out of it, but didn't do any good.

Approaching the gates of the cemetery I see that the driver is helping both women out of the limo. Good, glad to see that. I long to be the one helping Karlie through this very difficult time. Allowing her to fall apart in my arms at the funeral home was as close as I will ever get.

8

"Hey Roger. What brings you out this way?" I greet and shake hands with our family attorney as he gets out of his car in front of the 6AB.

"Hi Aiden, is your dad around? I need to meet with him and yourself if at all possible."

"Sure, let's go in the house. He'll be in there somewhere."

I lead him into my parents' living room and holler for Dad to come join us. Once he does, we all sit down and Roger gets down to business. I can't help but wonder what in the world he has to talk to us about.

"As you both know, I am the attorney for both the Blake and Doone families. Now that Gene has passed away, I'm trying to get all the ducks in a row for Ella Mae. As I am sure you are aware AJ, Gene had been investing in 6AB Breeds, your horse breeding program, and has a sizable portion of said company. He had asked that the ownership be passed onto Karlie and Jonathan once he was no longer able to be a part of it. Normally the wife receives the ownership, but this is something Gene specifically put in the will. After he had the first stroke, he made sure that all of his I's were crossed and T's were crossed."

"Ok, wait. You are saying that Karlie is now part owner of 6AB Breeds? And Jonathan?"

Yes son, Gene wanted to be a part of the place he has worked for around forty years. He's been a big part of the program from the beginning so I didn't have a problem in it when he asked me about being an owner also. We talked before we started the whole program and he has been the one that has run most of it anyway."

"Why didn't I know this? We have been doing the breeding program for almost ten years and I had no idea he was anything more than the head foreman here on the 6AB."

"Does it really matter Aiden? I didn't think you would object with it being Gene and all."

"No, of course not. I am just a little shocked. This is coming from left field."

"Aiden, your Dad and Gene thought that until they knew it was going to work, they kept it out of the public records, but once it was a success it was the least of their worries to change."

"That sounds reasonable. Do Ella Mae and Karlie know about this?"

Ella Mae does yes. Karlie, I am not sure about. I do know that Jonathan knows. Do you know AJ if Karlie knows about her new ownership?"

No, Gene didn't want Karlie to know about it. He didn't want her to feel obligated to come back to Colvin. She may think differently about it now. But I would be willing to buy out Gene's portion, well Karlie and Jonathan's portion, if that is what they decide to do. I know how much she doesn't want to live here and with Jonathan being in the military it may be what they decide."

"I would buy their portion in a heartbeat Dad. I guess one of us should go talk to her. Have you talked to her or Ella Mae about any of this yet?"

"No, I came to you first to see where your head was with all of this. I wanted to know if you were willing to buy them out if it came to that. I will give her that option. I am meeting them tomorrow and will get them up to speed. "

"Thanks for the heads up. Dad, do you want me to talk to Karlie or do you want to? She might receive it a little better from you than me."

"Ya, I will go talk to her right now. Been meaning to check on them today anyway. Not sure how long Karlie is going to be in town now with Ella Mae being alone."

"Don't look at me, I don't have a clue."

"Well then, I will talk to you after I meet with the ladies tomorrow. Have a good day gentlemen."

"You too. Thanks again for stopping by."

Well that was very strange. I haven't known this whole time that Gene was a business partner. I was the one who came up with the breeding program idea. Crazy. I still can't believe he didn't tell Karlie about it. I guess she wouldn't want to be tied down to Colvin, so why would he? Wait, they started this a couple eyars before we graduated from high school. Gene knew back then that Karlie would leave and not come back. Wish she did. Wish I would have known.

****

Knock Knock

"AJ, what a nice surprise. Please come in. Mom is in the living room looking at old photo albums. She has been doing that a lot since the funeral. I hope she gets better soon; I will feel so guilty going back to LA if she doesn't."

"Can we sit in the kitchen then? I need to discuss something with you, it doesn't concern her."

"Um, sure. Would you like something to drink?"

"I'm good thanks."

"What's up? Everyone ok?"

"Everyone and everything is fine. Karlie, your Dad and I are partners in 6AB Breeds. Did you know that?"

"No, how long has he been?"

"Since the start. I take it you didn't know anything?"

"No, but it sounds great though. So now Mom will get the ownership right? She will love having another excuse to visit the ranch and Amelia."

"No, Roger Yasser came by the ranch to talk to me earlier today because of the ownership change. Your Dad named you and your brother as the ones to inherit not your Mom. He knew she had her bakery and wouldn't want anything to do with the horses. Do you know if and when Jonathan will be home?"

"No, haven't heard a word. Wow. I am a little shocked here. I had no idea this whole time Dad owned part of the program. You started it before I was out of high school. Does Aiden know? I'm surprised he didn't tell me either."

"No, he didn't know until today either. We would like to offer you the option of buying your portion out if you don't want to continue on with it yourself. It takes extensive amounts of time and your Dad always took care of it. I will hire someone obviously not, but if you and Jonathan want to take it over, that is perfectly fine too."

"I don't know anything about breeding horses and I haven't a clue what Jonathan's plans are. I have my studio in LA too. I'll let you know as soon as I talk to him. I was afraid you were going to tell me something terrible."

"Is Aiden's being around going to have any influence on your decision?"

"No, why would it?"

"Your Dad and I always thought you two would get married and keep the 6AB and Blake name going. But, you left and we weren't sure what happened between you two. Then when you didn't come back all these years, we were afraid you being around each other would cause issues."

"Nah, we're adults. It's okay. I'm sure he is over me leaving by now anyways. I haven't seen him since the funeral and I doubt that I will again before I go back to LA."

"Well, no hurry. Nothing is changing out there that needs your immediate answer. It will just be you that gets the checks now. I will make sure we get your address to the attorney and he can set it all up for you."

"Thanks AJ. I will let you know as soon as I know something. Take care."

"Bye sweetheart. Come by and visit anytime. Do tell us goodbye this time." He winks and walks out the door which makes me smile. That is something that hasn't been easy this past week.

"I'll try. Give my best to the family. Bye."

Holy cow. I am part owner of the breeding program at 6AB. Wow. How did I not know this all these years? Poor Dad, I bet he didn't tell me because he thought I wouldn't want to be here. I guess he was right; I left and didn't come back until recently. What a terrible daughter I am. Wonder if Jonathan knows about this? What do I do about it now? I wish he would call me.

****

Dad has been gone now for six days and it just doesn't seem real. My heart aches more than I ever thought possible after laying my father to rest in that lonely cemetery.

Today is the start of a new life without the most loving and wonderful man I have ever known. Such a void in my life now.

There is only one place that I know where I can still feel his presence. At the creek where we went fishing and took pictures. Mom has her neighbor Cecelia here helping her so I sneak off for some alone time.

I swing by the liquor store first and get some champagne. A couple bottles should do. No glasses. This isn't a special occasion. Maybe the champagne will numb the aching inside or at least I will pass out and get more sleep than I have in days.

At the 6AB Ranch I take the well-known road that winds to the creek. There is a new gate where there never has been before. That's weird. I guess I'll climb over the gate. Walking will be good. I should have worn different shoes and not this dress. I take off the shoes and throw them in my car and proceed to climb over as best I can in this tight dress. If I were in any other shape I would care how ridiculous I must look to someone passing by, but right now I don't care at all. Not like anyone will see me clear out here.

After finally clearing that darn fence I start to see the road as I remember it. It winds around this way to the left and then oh wow it looks exactly the same as it did when I was young. I feel as though I could be watching a movie with all the memories that are shooting through my head. I haven't even had any alcohol yet.

At the creek's edge I sit where Dad and I always did on those hot summer days. The longer I stare at the water's edge, the more my heart hurts and the harder it is to breathe. The more tears that fall I realize that I don't know how to say goodbye. Goodbye to the greatest man I have ever known. Goodbye to the man who taught me to ride a bike, ride a horse, and most importantly to use a camera.

As I sit drinking my champagne I realize that I am on the second bottle and it makes me giggle. I have never drank this much, ever. But I have never been this upset or lost.

"Daddy, this was our special place and I will never forget it." I say between hiccups. "You were the best man I have ever met and I will miss you dearly every single day of the rest of my life. Thank you for all you have done for me. I will see you again one day and I will be so happy when that day comes."

"One of the best men you ever met." I hear from the other side of the creek. That deep familiar voice should startle me but it doesn't. It actually comforts me a little. It alleviates a bit of the ache inside as I hear it.

"Who says one of them? Who could be the other?" I say with a smile knowing his meaning.

"Can I come across and join you?" Aiden asks.

"Of course. It is your family's land. I'm the intruder."

"Actually, this is a part of my ranch. I bought a portion of it seven years ago." He says with a proud sound in his voice. "But you are always welcome here and never an intruder."

"This place feels the same but will never be the same. I can't believe he is gone." I drop my head into my hands and finally let the emotion out not feeling ashamed at all.

"I'm so sorry Karlie. He was a great man. Jonathan didn't make it back from Iraq I see. That's a shame." He says and sits down next to me on the creek bank while putting his arm around my shoulders. His touch makes me relax a little.

"They were to get a message to him but as far as we know he hasn't gotten it yet."

"He'll come back and it will get easier for you." He says softly as I lean into his side letting memories from our childhood overwhelm my senses. Sitting here exactly like this and talking about the future but at the same time I didn't know it was a future without

Aiden takes the bottle from my hand and inspects its label. He takes a big swig and dramatically spits it back out before saying, "Yuck, why are you drinking champagne?"

"Best I could find at the Triple E Liquor in town."

"Your tastes sure have changed. But all of you has changed." He says looking at me in the moonlight with eyes shining like the stars above.

"Been awhile Aiden. You, yourself, have changed. Look at you. All grown up and a ranch owner." I say trying not to look at his strong arms or chest. How can being this close to him affect me so strongly after all these years?

"Yep. Been over eight years. Eight long years."

"And now you're getting engaged. Congratulations." I choke out turning my head to hide the emotion written on my face.

"That's not set in stone. Not sure if I want that." He says unsure of the whole situation.

"That's not what Tracey thinks. You were just picking out rings with her not long ago Aiden."

"She wanted to look, I was simply pacifying her to get her off my back about it. She wants it, but I'm not sure. What about you? Things used to seem so simple back when we were kids. We used to be such a good team. Before you left and never came back."

"I couldn't come back Aiden. Being around you was going to be too hard. I didn't have a choice but to leave."

"Karlie you left me, remember? You were ashamed of what we did. I thought it was the best night of my life and went to tell you just that the next morning but you left early for LA." He declares turning me back to face him with a stern look on his face.

"I wasn't ashamed Aiden; you were the one who regretted it. You looked so pained on the drive back to my house and I loved you so much. I left as soon as I could to save you the shame."

"No Karlie, I was so in love with you it hurt. I knew you were leaving and I wasn't sure if I would ever see you again." He says reaching for my hand. "Looks like we both thought wrong. Now eight years have gone by and a lot of wasted time."

I hiccup and stand up to leave, but my legs are like noodles from all the alcohol I've drank. I fall but Aiden catches me just like he did that night we were out here and made love. This feeling of his arms wrapped around me is what I have been looking and waiting for. For eight years. I can't have Dad's arms around me anymore, but Aiden's are the next best thing.

"You can't drive Karlie; you can stay at my house. There is plenty of room." He says before he can change his mind and stands us both up.

"You really loved me?" I ask between hiccups as I let him help me to the vehicle. "Why didn't you ever tell me?"

"Same reason you didn't tell me. I was afraid you wouldn't feel the same and our friendship would get all weird." I hear him say before passing out.

****

Karlie is asleep by the time we make it the short distance to the house. I pull the pickup into the garage and walk around to her side to wake her up. She still can't hold her alcohol. That makes me smile knowing she hasn't changed too much from the Karlie Mae I knew growing up.

She loved me too. How could I not have known that? We could have been married this whole time and have a house full of kids. She looks so peaceful and so beautiful. As I lift her out of the pickup seat I fight my own guilt and emotions about our talk earlier. She thought I was ashamed. I thought she was ashamed. What a mess.

I walk to the guest room to put Karlie into the bed but I realize it isn't made up. So, I take her to my bedroom. She can sleep in here and I will make up the guest room. I walk through the door of my bedroom and realize I have never had Karlie in my bedroom. Having Karlie in my bed was one of the biggest dreams I had growing up and now it's happening. But I can't touch her like that. I can't love her like that. But I do love her.

As I lay her down she reaches for me and calls out my name in her sleep. I can't help but let my heart do as she asks. I used to do exactly this when we were kids and she was upset about something. We both know she is beyond upset tonight and this is probably not a good idea. An idea I can't put out of my mind.

So, I lay down with her vowing to stay only until she goes back to a deep sleep. But as I lay down beside Karlie I can't help but feel at home and at peace.

She curls herself into me and I am struck with how real and good this feels. I, myself, have had a long day and can't keep my eyes open. Before long we are both asleep. Together in each other's arms.

****

"What is going on here?" I hear a woman scream from somewhere in the room.

As I come to, I realize that I am still lying in my bed but Karlie is in my arms and we are intertwined like a pretzel. My heart registers the fact that we stayed close and comfortable all night like this. But then my head clears and reminds me that this wasn't what was supposed to happen.

And now Tracey is standing at the end of the bed very upset. Oh boy. I scramble out of bed as quick as I can trying not to wake Karlie up. She needs her rest and will need the extra sleep when the hangover starts from all that nasty champagne she drank.

"Tracey, it's not what it looks like. Karlie was upset and drinking so I brought her back here to sleep it off and I guess I fell asleep too." I say as quickly as I can trying to usher her out of the room and away from Karlie. "We have never been anything more than good friends." I know that was a lie, but what other choice did I have in this situation?

"I don't know what else to say Aiden. I come back from being out of town to find my boyfriend in bed with another woman. I thought you loved me!" I put my arms around her

and pull her body against mine. She doesn't deserve this.
It's not her fault I am so darn confused.

"I'm so sorry Tracey; it will never happen again I
promise we are just friends." I say and kiss her reluctant lips.
And just as I do that I hear footsteps in the kitchen.

****

Pulling myself out of bed, I realize that I am still at
Aiden's and need to get out of here. I only vaguely
remember our conversation last night but it's not something I
want to delve into right now. My head is killing me. I make
my way towards voices and can see it's Aiden and Tracey
having a bit of an argument as I enter the room.

Just a friend huh? Wow so that is how he feels about
me. Yes, I should have known. He is going to marry her
and have the life we were meant to have. Have the children
we were supposed to have.

"Um, can I get a ride to my car? I left it by the gate on
the creek road." I ask quietly hoping not to start another fight

and unable to look at Aiden knowing he would be able to read my face and know what I was thinking.

"I will take you. I have errands to run in town anyway. Bye Aiden. Talk to you later." Tracey says as she plants a whopper of a kiss on his lips. All for my benefit I am sure. She can have him. She is what he wants anyways.

"Thanks." I say and move to the door not daring look at either of them.

As we climb into her car she asks, "You still love him don't you?"

"I care about him a lot yes, but not sure it's love. He is with you anyway, why does it matter?" I say back feeling defeated and unable to look at her.

"He is with me and we are going to get married someday soon. I am really sorry to hear about your Dad. He was a nice man. Always helped me find Aiden when I came to the parents' ranch." She said curtly knowing she was getting under my skin.

The parents' ranch? She acts as if they are already married. Whatever. This life isn't for me, it's for Tracey. I don't remember this road being this long. Thank goodness we are about there. To my car. My ticket back to my life. Without Aiden. In LA or Colvin? With Jeremy? Boy do I have a headache.

9

A few days after that awkward walk of shame or whatever it was, I decide that it's time to figure out what it is I am going to do now with KAB and my career. I know Mom needs me here but I also know that I can't just sit around doing nothinI need something to take my mind off of my relationship issues. Or lack thereof.

I have been walking up and down this commercial district of Colvin now for a few hours hoping to see a sign that I should be relocating myself and KAB here. I sit on a bench in the town square when I see a bubbly blond walking towards me with a huge smile on her face that looks so familiar. Once she says my name I know it's Savannah. I haven't seen her either since I left.

"Karlie Mae Doone!! What are you doing? Are you back here?" she asks throwing her arms around me just like she used to when we were younger.

"I have been here since right after Dad had the first stroke. What are you doing here? I didn't think you lived here anymore!" I say genuinely happy to see a familiar face.

"I'm here for a meeting at my parents' attorney's office. Mom and Dad divorced earlier this year and I am being their go between. I live in Miami with my husband and two boys but had to fly here yesterday to take care of the last piece of their settlement. They finally sold the house here and wanted to split it halfway but neither wants to see the other, so here I am." She says looking annoyed. "I am so sorry to hear about your Dad."

"Thank you. It has been rough but we're getting by. I didn't know you lived in Miami! How exciting. I did a shoot there a couple years ago. It's so full of life." I say remembering how fast paced that city was.

"How long are you staying now?" she asks leaning back on the bench we now shared. "Where are you living and what's been up in your life since graduation? We lost touch."

I go into the story since I last saw her not leaving anything out which kind of surprised me. She just nodded at the right times and commented when needed like the polite person she is. It felt really good to talk to a person outside my world. I also realized that I really don't have anyone but my Mom and of course Gerry when he isn't on location or sending me on one. It would be so great to have a friend again to share things with. Of course my mind can't help but wander to Aiden again. I shake my head and push him to the back again. Where he needs to stay.

"So, have you seen Aiden since you have been back? You two used to be so close. I take it you aren't now?"

"I have seen him yes, but he has a girlfriend and is talking about getting engaged. I don't fit in his life anymore so I have been trying to avoid seeing him anymore than is needed."

"Well, have you found anything here that feels like the new KAB? There is that small space above your Mom's bakery shop. Have you thought about that? It would be a great space with great light and you would be close to her." She says sounding as if she just solved the world's problems.

I had to laugh at her excitement but realized that she may be right. Mom just uses that space as storage. Maybe I should talk to Mom about it. We say our good-byes and exchange contact info so we can keep in touch this time. It was really good seeing and talking to Savannah again. She hasn't changed much.

****

"Mom, I need to talk to you." I say walking into the store not knowing that Aiden's Mom was there "Oh, Amelia, I didn't know you were here."

"Hi sweet girl. How are you?" Amelia says giving me a hug the size of Texas. Amelia always was like a second mother to me whenever I was with Aiden at the 6AB Ranch.

"I missed you guys too, believe me. So what are you two up to?" I say trying to push the tears and emotion back. I don't want them to know I am upset and especially not about Aiden.

"We are working on the fundraiser for the library. It's this Saturday. You are still planning on taking the pictures for us aren't you?" Mom declares and I nod my head as a yes.

"Speaking of taking pictures, Aiden has kept me in the loop on your life over the years. He always knows the latest accomplishment you have or where your latest shoot was taking place." I know what she is doing. She always did know when he and I were at odds.

"What do you mean? Mom did you tell him everything?"

"Your Mom didn't say anything. He always followed everything you did or asked your father about you. I believe he has always loved you Karlie."

"But he is with Tracey talking marriage." I say hurt and not trying to hide it this time.

"She is talking marriage, he isn't. Or at least not to me. I don't believe he truly loves Tracey the way he thinks he does or should."

"You need to talk to him Karlie Mae. Before you go back and start talking about your future with Jeremy." Mom says while turning me and making me look into her eyes.

"Oh, so there is another man in the picture too? I wasn't aware. Does Aiden know?" Amelia asks shocked.

"Yes, Jeremy is great. And no, Aiden doesn't know. He told Tracey we were just friends anyway, so he doesn't need to know." I continue on to fill her in on the whole scenario before walking out of the room. I have to put distance between myself and anything Aiden related.

"He was caught in a tough spot that's all." She yells after me.

Whatever. I will move on too. With Jeremy. With Jeremy? I will move on from Aiden for sure. As long as I never see him I will be strong and it will be easier.

****

"Aiden Steven Blake, we need to talk!" I hear Mom yell from the front door. "Where are you young man?"

Uh oh she used my full name and young man in the same breath. What did I do now? "In the office Mom." I say smiling and remembering being a child and hating to hear her do that.

As she enters the room I am shutting down my laptop and closing it to allow her my full attention which she will expect of me. "What can I do for you mother?"

"What were you thinking telling Tracey that you and Karlie are just friends? We all know you are much more than that!"

"What are you talking about?"

"You told Tracey that you and Karlie are just friends the morning after the funeral. I know Karlie stayed there with you and you two fell asleep in your bed by accident." She says trying not to look so pleased by that.

"How in the world do you know about that? We were alone in the kitchen while Karlie was... Oh no, she heard us didn't she?" I say starting to make sense of all of this.

"Yes son, she did! And it broke her heart into a million little pieces. Then she had to hear all that Tracey could throw at her on the short trip from your house to her car at the gate. How could you have let this happen? Have you even spoken to Karlie since she left here that morning?"

"Mom I didn't know Karlie was near enough to hear me. And I didn't know what else to tell Tracey. It just kind of came out. It is the truth though. We aren't anything more than that technically. I was in a tough spot after Tracey found us. And I made it much worse. No I haven't seen her since then." I say defeated and sit down in my chair again.

As I do I see the picture of Karlie and I on the horse with her Dad that was used at the funeral. I sure have made another mess where Karlie is concerned. Seems to be the story of my life when it comes to her.

"You had better make this right son. Or you might lose your chance with her forever." With that she walks back out my office door and soon I hear the front door open and close.

I sigh deeply and spin my chair around to see Mom speeding away in a cloud of dust. Once I can't see her any longer I walk over to the picture and pick it up. Things were so much less complicated back then. What am I supposed to do to fix this?

10

The next day I am helping Mom out in the store when I hear her from behind the counter say, "Karlie, our neighbor Cecelia just called and says you need to go home because something just showed up for you."

I put the final touch on the pumpkin cookie order we had from Audrey Blake which is the 2nd grade teacher here in town and say. "What showed up? I wasn't expecting anything."

"She didn't say, just that you might want to come get it now. I will box these up and be home in a few also. Thank you for doing these. Audrey will love them."

As I walk to Mom's house I can't seem to guess what has arrived for me. I really didn't order anything so what could it be? As I come around the corner of our block, I see that there is a strange car in the drive way. Who in the world could that be? Maybe Gerry came to see me about a new shoot. Knowing it is probably Gerry I start to walk a bit faster.

Opening up the front door and catching the first glimpse of my mystery arrival, I come to a dead halt.

"Jeremy, what are you doing here? I thought you had a business trip to New Orleans?" I say and run to him. As he pulls me into his arms it dawns on me that I haven't seen him or talked to him too much since I have been here and since Dad passed away.

"I came to surprise you. You were the trip I had to take. I just couldn't tell you it was Colvin or it would have spoiled the surprise." He says as he kisses my forehead. "Your Mom told me it would be unlocked and to just come in."

"Mom knew you were coming? Wow. When did you talk to my Mom?" I ask suddenly not feeling too happy about this. "How did you get her number?"

"Yes she knew I was coming and I got her number off the internet. Are you not happy that I am here?"

"Yes I'm happy to see you, I'm just shocked. You have been so busy over these past couple of months that I didn't expect to see you here. In Colvin, especially."

"Where can I put my things? Your room?" he says winking at me.

"You can stay in the spare bedroom. I don't think it would be appropriate for you to stay with me while my Mom is around." I say motioning towards the spare bedroom down the hall from mine.

"Ok I can understand that. Lead the way. She isn't going to be home for awhile is she?"

"Here you go. She said she would be right behind me so I am sure she is about here." I say hoping I was right. Mom would definitely put a damper on Jeremy's plans for this bedroom.

Just as he turned and tried to pin me against the wall, I hear the front door open and close. Must be Mom, right on time.

"That's Mom. Come on I will introduce you formally before dinner." I say grabbing his hand and rushing out of the room towards where Mom stood in the kitchen. "Mom, this mysterious arrival is Jeremy Bander. I guess you already knew that though."

"Nice to finally meet you ma'am. I see where Karlie gets her beauty from. Thank you so much for allowing me to surprise her today. You were very helpful." Jeremy says as he kisses Mom's hand.

"It was my pleasure. My Karlie deserves to have a special someone and if I can help get him here, I sure will. Welcome. What would you like for dinner?" Mom says and I swear she blushed as he kissed her hand.

"Mrs. Doone I would like to take you and Karlie out to dinner tonight. Is there a nice restaurant here in town?" he asks.

"Please, call me Ella Mae. Mrs. Doone was my mother in law. There is only a café here Jeremy. But we can still go there if you would like. Probably nothing close to what you are used to in LA."

"A nice little café would be a wonderful change of pace. What do you think Karlie?"

"Sure, if that's what you two want." I realize I am being a bit over dramatic here. He has come all this way to see me I should enjoy it. It wasn't too long ago that I was practically begging him to come here and now that he is I should be grateful. "Let Mom and I go change. Then we will be ready."

"Mind if I go with you babe? We have so much to catch up on." Jeremy says without a hint of mischief.

"Sure. See you in a few Mom. My room is this way." I lead him towards my room. "It's kind of a mess from packing up old stuff to give away to charity but it allows me to sleep. That's all that I need right?"

"Baby why do you seem so nervous to be around me? Aren't you happy I came to see you?" he says and wraps his arms around me. "I have missed you so much."

"I've missed you too, it's just that so much has happened here and I'm not the same person I was before I came here." I say and relax against his chest. I really have missed him and his arms around me. Maybe this is a good thing.

Before I can make that decision Jeremy lifts my head up to his and kisses me softly. "I am so sorry I couldn't make it for the funeral Karlie. I was so swamped and deadlines were looming. I feel terrible though."

After a long passionate kiss I catch my breath and say, "It really is ok Jeremy. You are very busy and I know that. I hadn't been back here for so many years either because of being so busy. I am definitely one to understand. But you are here now and that's all that matters."

"You had better get changed so we can go. I am starving and haven't eaten since an early breakfast at the office. Can't wait to see what this little place is like where you grew up. Will you show me around after dinner?" he asks and kisses me again.

"Sure, but there isn't much to it. Won't take long."

****

Entering Sally's Café with Mom and Jeremy felt strange. Everyone had finally quit giving us that "oh you poor things" look and Dad's passing was old news. Norma, Sally's sister points towards my favorite booth with a smile. I smile back and slide in on one side followed by Jeremy. Mom takes her seat across from us. I can see there are stars in her eyes and she's hearing wedding bells. Great, he has only been here an hour and Mom is planning the wedding.

"Well Karlie and Ella Mae! So good to see you two! How are you doing? And who is this handsome devil with you Karlie Mae? Wow." Norma says as she hands us our menus, always cutting right to the chase.

"Hi Norma, we are good. This is my boyfriend Jeremy Bander from LA. I will have my normal and I'm sure Mom will, too. Do you see anything you want Jeremy?" I say handing the menu back to Norma.

"Do you need more time, Handsome?" Norma asks with reddening cheeks and a crooked smile.

I forgot how good looking Jeremy is with his high cheek bones, sexy mouth, green eyes, and jet black hair cut short.

"I'll have a chicken fried steak, mashed potatoes, and green beans. With an iced tea to drink, please." He says and hands his menu to Norma and winks. That gets even more color in her cheeks.

"Coming right up!" She says and winks back at Jeremy.

"Friendly in this town, I see. If I weren't already taken I bet I could get a date with Norma over there." He says laughing and wrapping his left arm around me tightly. "But thank goodness I am taken."

"Everyone is nice here yes, I'm just glad you came to see Karlie. How long are you staying Jeremy?" Mom asks with a smile.

"I have a plane to catch to New Orleans tomorrow afternoon. So I guess a little less than 24 hours." He says reluctantly and squeezes my shoulder. "I knew I needed to stop off here on my way to see you."

"Glad you did." I say before my gaze fell to a familiar blond hair and blue eyed man that just came through the café door.

With another blond and blue beauty beside him. Aiden and Tracey just had to come in here now. Lightening strike me now please.

I look away and try to pretend I didn't just get butterflies seeing another man other than my boyfriend walk in the door. A man other than the one sitting next to me. It would be even harder if he wasn't here though. Then I would see Aiden and be sitting here alone while he had his girlfriend with him. We are "just friends" anyway, so he says. Why does it bother me so much to see him? I am over him.

"Hi Ella Mae, Karlie. How are you ladies?" I hear his words breaking me out of my inner tantrum.

"Oh, Aiden and Tracey it's so nice to see you. This is Jeremy Bander, Karlie's boyfriend from LA. He has stopped off to see us on his way to New Orleans." Mom says sounding so proud.

"Oh, planning on some fun?" Aiden says with a voice laced with sarcasm and dislike.

"No, I am headed there on a business trip. My company is helping in the rebuilding of some of the damaged Katrina areas. We do nonprofit work like that all around the world wherever we are needed." Jeremy says knowing his credentials would knock the socks off of the country bumpkin Aiden was acting like.

"Well, that's great. Nice to see you all." Aiden says and tries to catch eyes with me but I look away and lay my head on Jeremy's shoulder. Aiden wants to be just friends; well I will treat him that way too.

****

She has a boyfriend. And he's successful. Great. No wonder she is so mad at me and doesn't love me like I do her. I live in small town Colvin and own a ranch. This guy has so much more to offer her than I do. Can I blame her?

"Karlie's boyfriend is quite the looker." Tracey says as we sit down at the table Norma showed us to. "They seem in love too."

"Yep. Happy for them." I lie and bury myself in the all too familiar menu while stewing over seeing her sitting there with her head on another man's shoulder. That should be my shoulder.

I messed that up though. Like always. I will never get a chance with her now. I thought I was going to talk to Tracey today about breaking up but I can see this isn't the time. Maybe I'm supposed to be with her and not Karlie.

"You are quiet again Aiden. What's wrong?" Tracey asks and caresses my hand. "You don't like Karlie's boyfriend do you?"

"Don't be silly. She isn't my concern. I just hope he isn't out to take advantage of poor Ella Mae in her grieving state." I say sharply not caring how ridiculous that all just sounded.

"Enough of that, are we going to the fundraiser Saturday at the 6AB?" Tracey asks and slides out of the booth and holds her hand out for me to follow.

"Of course I am. Are you wanting to go too?" I ask hoping her answer is no.

"Yes Aiden. I would love to go with you." She smiles and walks towards the door as I hand Norma cash for our bill.

I just pray this city slicker is gone by then. I don't want him traipsing around the 6AB and getting his hooks in any deeper into the Doone women. Especially Karlie.

****

After eating our fill and talking our fill too, Jeremy and I head off to walk around town together.

"This is a very peaceful place. I don't understand how you could leave it behind for the fast paced world of LA." Jeremy says as we walk into the town square and see the lights start to come on all around us as it gets dark out. "It's literally like night and day."

"I don't remember it being like this at all when I was young. It's definitely not what I had pictured. I have taken so many pictures of just simple things since I got here. It's been so easy to get lost in the subject matter and forget

where I am. I could never have done that before I left." I say
and hug Jeremy tighter to me. "I really am glad you came."

"I have really missed you Karlie. It's been so tough not
being able to talk to you. We have played phone tag for
weeks. I just couldn't go any longer without talking to you
in person. Seeing this beautiful face and kissing these soft
lips." He says and kisses me like never before. He really did
miss me and I'm thankful I still get those butterflies when he
kisses me.

"I have missed you too. This past couple of weeks has
been the most difficult of my life. I am so glad I came
though. I can't imagine not being here when Dad passed
away. Mom would have been alone." I say and shiver
knowing how terrible that would have been.

"Karlie, you knew what you needed to do. Now, do you
think you could come home? Your Mom seems good and
you seem at peace also. I miss being able to hold you and
kiss you whenever I want to." He says pulling me closer
again.

"I hadn't really thought about when I was leaving again. I guess just getting through day by day has been my plan." Slipping out of his arms I walk to the fountain in the center of the park and sit on the ledge. "I'm not sure I want to leave, Jeremy. I really don't know."

"Babe, you can do whatever you want. I want you to come home, of course. You could always move your Mom out there now that she is alone and we can get her set up with a new store. Then we can be together but you can still have your Mom nearby. I have something I brought for you." He says and kneels down on one knee and pulls a small blue box out of his jacket pocket. That little blue box that every girl in LA dreams of getting.

"Jeremy, what are you doing?" I ask starting to panic with the thought of what his next words will be.

"Karlie Doone, I love you and want to spend the rest of our lives together. Will you make me happy and be my wife?" he asks with a smile so sweet and sure.

I freeze and start to feel faint. I'm not sure I can answer. Do I answer with yes when I haven't a clue what I want or who I even am anymore? "Jeremy, I can't answer that right now. I told you that before I left I wasn't sure I could get married yet. So much has happened and I really don't know any better than I did before. I'm sorry that you came all this way for this but I just can't answer you right now."

With that answer I run towards home in tears. I have never been so confused and lost in my life. What am I supposed to do now? Once I open the front door and see Mom sitting in her chair reading like she always has, it hits me that she knew that was going to happen.

"Mom! How could you not warn me? You of all people should know that I have changed a lot since I left here all those years ago. I have even changed so much more since I have come back! I don't know what I want!" I say and run to my room slamming the door behind me hoping to shut the world and everyone in it out.

****

I must have cried myself to sleep because as I come to I see that the sun is streaming in the windows in my room and I have a massive headache and dry mouth. Still clad in my clothes from the night before, I head to the kitchen. I just pray Mom has made coffee and there is some left.

As I enter the kitchen though I see that Mom isn't happy with me. She's standing next to the sink with a sour look on her face and tapping her nails on the counter.

"Well, nice to see you come out of your room young lady. In there pouting like you were six again." Mom says sharply.

"Where is Jeremy?" I ask quickly trying to change the subject.

"He left last night Karlie after you ran away from his proposal. He was so hurt when he got back here. He packed up his things and asked me to give you this letter when you woke up. You really messed up girl." Mom says with a frown, hands me the letter, and walks out the front door.

I get a cup of coffee and sit on the nearest barstool and open the envelope, let out a big sigh and begin to read his words.

Dearest Karlie,

As we both know, you are a very wonderful woman and I love you very much. I know that me not being here for you these past few weeks has been very hard on you. I should have come sooner, and for that I am sorry. You will never know just how sorry.

I never thought you wouldn't answer my proposal. I thought I was doing what the next step needed to be in our relationship. I guess I was wrong.

I have gone onto New Orleans early to give you some time to think all of this over and give you space. I still want to marry you and will be awaiting

your answer.

I love you,

Jeremy

He left. He just left without a word. What did I expect? He laid it out there and I didn't answer. What a fool I was. And cruel. What do I do now?

Mom is obviously happy about the proposal. She probably has the wedding all planned out down to the last detail. Why couldn't I just say yes? Jeremy is great and I do love him. Why didn't I answer? I just ran away like a school girl.

11

It has been a couple of days since Jeremy was here and with every day I feel worse. But today is the fundraiser Mom has been working so hard on with Amelia. They are raising money to help the library in town get new books and a few upgrades done inside. I agreed to take pictures even though I know it's at the 6AB Ranch. Which means Aiden will be there. With Tracey. If it didn't mean so much to my Mom and Amelia I wouldn't be doing it. I vowed to move on from him. And I am.

I am setting up my equipment when AJ comes over to say hello. As I watch him approach, I realize he is a really big guy. Anyone who doesn't know him would be intimidated but I step right into his arms for the AJ bear hug I have always gotten and loved.

"Hey sweetie, how's it going?" he asks. "How are you and your mama getting along these days?"

"Things are going as good as they can since Dad passed away but it's getting easier. Thanks." I say back feeling comforted for the first time since I was with Aiden at the creek. This is the closest to a father's hug I will ever get again and that makes me so sad.

As I step out of his arms I see Aiden and Tracey arriving and we catch each other's gaze. I tell AJ that I have lots of work to do and turn my back on the rest of the group. I have got to get myself in check. This might be harder than I thought.

"Hey Karlie, I was hoping you would take a picture of Aiden and I together?" I hear Tracey say from behind me. Crap. Things just got even harder.

I turn, smile and say politely, "Sure, let's go over here where the light is better and the background can be that old tree. Where is Aiden?"

"Aiden! Honey! Karlie is going to take our picture!" She yells to him and he comes over definitely not looking like he is excited about this. Those feelings are mutual.

"Ok, get closer and lean back a little bit towards the tree. Smile." I say wanting to scream and throw a tantrum. Just as I do Tracey pulls Aiden over to her and plants a steamy kiss on his lips as I snap the photo. Great now I will forever have proof of losing him.

"Thanks. I would like a copy of that one." She says and drags him off, literally dragging him away. I could tell he wanted to talk to me but found it easier to be dragged off. Which works for me.

****

Karlie looks so happy behind the camera. She knows how to get what she wants to come out the other end of it for sure. I can't help but smile as I see her snapping pictures of all the kids and parents. She was always so at ease behind the lens of the camera. I bet after Tracey's dumb photo idea she is upset.

"And my little Karlie will be going back to LA soon where she has a special man who has asked her to be his wife. So I may have something to celebrate soon." I overhear Ella Mae saying to the fundraiser guests.

That makes my stomach turn. Knowing Karlie could be another man's wife makes me dizzy. How could this all happen? I have to talk to her. I saw her heading to the barn with her camera. I am sure I will find her in the foal's pen where she always went before.

"Thought I would find you here." I say walking to the pen "I'm really sorry about that stunt she pulled. Did you get any good shots up there at all?"

"Hi Aiden. Yes, I believe I did. Ran out of things to photograph though. Hope you don't mind." She says politely not looking at me.

"You know my parents won't mind. They have always loved you like a 5th child Karlie." I say looking at her as she turns her face towards me.

"Thank you. That means a lot." She says and looks away. Emotion written all over her face that hits me like a punch to the gut.

"Karlie, I am so sorry about you overhearing what I said to Tracey the other morning. I have never told anyone about our night together and I didn't feel that was the time either. She was so upset and I just wanted to calm her down. She didn't believe me that nothing happened. I didn't know you heard me until my mother came and chewed me out after talking to you. I really am sorry." I say hoping she believes me. I want so bad to grab her hands or even kiss her.

"It's okay Aiden. We aren't more than friends. One night back then doesn't change anything. We were kids. We are adults now. If we had known we loved each other back then, things would definitely be different. We will never know." She says and I can see the hurt in her eyes that she is trying to mask.

"So, your Mom says you are going to be getting married soon? To that guy from Sally's? What's his name?" I ask. "Why didn't you tell me about him the other night by the creek?"

"Jeremy asked that night after seeing you in Sally's but I haven't answered. I didn't know he was even coming here, let alone that he was planning on proposing." She says quickly. "When are you going to propose to Tracey? She sure is lovely."

"I'm not sure. It just seems like something is missing and I can't figure it out." I say rubbing my hands over my face.

"I completely understand how you feel. That's why I told Jeremy I would answer after I came back from Colvin." She declares.

We stare at each other a minute then she says, "I need to get going. Goodbye Aiden. Good luck with Tracey." And she rushes by me and out of the barn.

I stay sitting on a bale of hay with my head in my hands when I hear footsteps. I look up to see my parents come in holding hands. Seeing them so happy after all these years warms my heart and makes me long for that for myself.

"Hey guys, what are you doing?"

"We saw Karlie leave in a hurry and pack her stuff up. We thought we might find you here." Dad says and sits beside me.

"She said goodbye to me and good luck with Tracey. She's going to get married." I say full of hurt and defeat while I just hang my head.

"It's time for you to choose between Tracey and Karlie son. We know you think you love Tracey but son from the Moment Gene brought little Karlie out here when you were five years old, we have seen the bond and known you two were meant to be together." Mom says trying not to cry. She takes my hands and hugs me hard. "We know you have loved Karlie your whole life. And still do."

"I didn't know anyone knew about my feelings for Karlie. She doesn't." I say in shock stepping back from Mom.

"Son we have always known that you both love each other more than life itself. You two are soul mates." Dad says with more emotion than I remember him showing before. Dad is talking about soul mates? What is going on around here?

As Mom and Dad turn to walk away I see the love in the touches they give each other and I realize that I want all of that and more. And I want it with Karlie. Not Tracey. That really hits me like a ton of bricks.

"You are right, I need to talk to her but I have to talk to Tracey first." I say with a broad smile as they walk away. "Thank you so much."

I walk back to the gathering and straight to where Tracey is.

"Tracey I need to get you home. There has been an emergency on the ranch I need to deal with." I say quickly and usher her into the pickup. I need to get this over with before I lose my nerve.

After a long and silent trip into town Tracey leads me into her apartment and says with a defeated look on her face, "It's Karlie, isn't it? The emergency is Karlie. I saw her running from the barn. You still love her don't you? I should have known. Audrey told me you might not be over her but I thought I could change your mind."

"Tracey I am so sorry. I thought I was ready to move on but I'm just not. You are a beautiful and wonderful woman, just not the woman meant for me. I hope you understand." I never meant to hurt Tracey. I have tried to make her happy but once Karlie came back I just couldn't keep my concentration on Tracey alone. I actually feel better than I have in a very long time but I have work to finish on the AK before dark. I will find Karlie in the morning first thing and tell her how I feel about her.

****

This makeshift dark room in the spare bathroom works just fine sealing out the world and leaving me in the one place that no one can see my pain. While developing all the photos from the fund raiser I see a photo of Aiden smiling towards Tracey. That is the last sliver that kept my heart from breaking in pieces. I know that I want to find someone to look at me that way but I also know I have to tell Jeremy I can't marry him either. I just don't feel that way for him.

"Jeremy, it's Karlie. I'm good. You? How is New Orleans? Good. Yes, Mom is good. She is actually adjusting better than I expected. I'm not sure if I'm ready to leave her alone Jeremy. No, she has her bakery store here and wouldn't leave. I am thinking of relocating KAB here. Yes, there is a space above Mom's store that I could clean out and use. I haven't talked to her about it yet, but I know she would be behind it if that's what I want. No, I don't know what I want for sure. I'm sorry Jeremy; I know you are hurting too. Yes, I have thought about your proposal but I can't marry you. I can't keep you on the side hoping I will change my mind. It isn't fair to you. Yes, I am sure and have thought a lot about it. Please just remember you are a great man and any woman would be so lucky to have you. One that isn't such a mess like me. Have a good life Jeremy and be happy. Thank you. Good-bye."

After talking to Jeremy, I feel lighter and ready to move on knowing I did the right thing for both of us. I am hoping for time alone to collect my thoughts and figure out my next move. But the doorbell rings breaking me out of my little dark room refuge.

"Hi Audrey, what are you doing here?" I ask as I open the door. Very shocked to see Aiden's sister on my doorstep. "Did something happen after I left? Is my mother okay?"

"No, I came to talk to you. Oh this photo of Aiden is great. Did you take it today? He looks so happy." Audrey says as she sees the photo in my hands. I must have forgotten to put it back on the line before I went to answer the door.

"Yes, he is looking at Tracey with all the love that a man should have for the woman he is going to marry." I say looking away hiding my pain but she steps forward and grabs my arm turning me back around.

"You are so wrong Karlie. He wasn't looking at Tracey. He was looking at you in the mirror. Look a little closer. You will see." She says pointing to the background. "He has never looked at anyone like that but you Karlie. And I don't think he ever will."

"Oh my goodness you are right. Wait, you are Tracey's best friend. Shouldn't you be mad?" I ask questioning and waiting for the next words from her not sure what direction this was going to go.

"No, I want what is best for my brother first. And he has loved you his whole life Karlie. Tracey will be fine. Go find him and talk to him please. Put us all out of our misery having to watch you two mope around." She says smiling and giving me a big hug.

"Thank you, Audrey. I owe you big." I grab my keys and run to my car feeling like a love sick teenager again.

****

Driving towards the ranch I see Aiden's pickup at an apartment building on the right. I slow my car down and see shadows on the window of a man and woman in an embrace. Something slams into my gut and I realize that I was being foolish. He doesn't love me at all. He loves Tracey and everyone else was wrong too. How could I let this happen again?

He wouldn't be at her house if he wanted to be with me. As reality comes flying back at me, I turn around in tears and head for Mom's. I run into the house and pack my clothes not wanting to explain. I can't stay here any longer. This is the reason I left here all those years ago and never came back. Here I am leaving the same way I did eight years ago.

Hurt and in love with Aiden. How could I be so foolish twice?

Driving to the airport this time feels different. This time I know how Aiden feels about me. The broken heart is the same but I also know I will survive it. I have to.

12

"Aiden, hello. What can I do for you?" Ella Mae asks as she opens the door the next morning. "Karlie isn't here if that's what you were hoping. She left late last night for LA."

"She didn't...." I say with so much emotion Ella Mae flinched. "Why did she leave so quickly? She didn't tell me she was leaving."

"She went to find you last night but saw you at Tracey's. She knows you picked Tracey, Aiden." Ella Mae says with tears welling up in her eyes.

"But she is wrong. I was breaking it off with Tracey. I love Karlie with all my being. I want to spend the rest of my life with her." I say wiping my own tears away. I never cry but this whole situation just rips my heart out again. She left me again. How could this be happening again?

"Oh you two are hopeless!! Always having the wrong assumptions. I don't know what happened between you two the night before she left eight years ago but I have never seen her so happy and miserable at the same time."

"I have always known that I loved your daughter and was going to marry her but when she left without a look or call back I thought that was what she wanted and that she didn't feel the same about me."

"She was afraid of getting stuck in this town and being a nobody. Little did she know she was a very special somebody. Especially to you." Ella Mae says lightly as she pulls me into a hug. "Isn't it about time you tell her that?"

"I'm going to right now." I say quickly as I head out the door. "And I won't come back without her!" I see the smile spreading across her face and hands me a piece of paper with Karlie's LA address on it. She is as happy as I feel. I just pray her daughter feels the same.

"Aaron, can I use your company jet to fly after Karlie? She left for LA last night. Yes, again. I know. This time I am going after her with a little surprise, well maybe not little, from that jeweler on Booker Ave. in Tulsa."

****

Home Sweet Home. Isn't that what they say? For some reason this apartment doesn't feel like home. It just feels empty and lonely. How did I live here for eight years? Alone. Maybe I spent too much time at Mom's and this feels so foreign because of it.

Speaking of Mom, I need to call her to let her know I got home okay. "Hi Mom, I made it home. I think you should come stay with me for a while. Going to miss you too. Love you." That was a quick conversation with Mom. Quickest ever. Strange. She must have been busy at the shop. I usually can't get her off the phone. Maybe she has had enough of me.

I know someone who will be happy to hear from me regardless. "Hey, Gerry. Yep, I am back. Fiji huh? Yes, I will do it. When do I leave? Wow so soon? Ok. I'll be looking for the email. Bye."

I'm going to Fiji for my next shoot tomorrow. That should be far enough away from Colvin and this hurt. Far enough away to help get Aiden off of my mind and out of my broken heart again. Will I ever get far enough though?

I change my clothes and unpack before checking my answering machine. I have one message. That's it? I just laugh. Of course one. Who would call me at home? Only one person ever did.

"Hello babe. I know you said you couldn't marry me but I think you are just upset about your Dad. I love you and want to spend the rest of my life with you. Please give us another chance after you get home from Oklahoma. I will be

at the condo until the 16th then I head to Boston until the

1st. Hope to see you soon."

I replay the message a few times before erasing it and sit on the bar stool in the kitchen. I wait for the tears to start falling but none seem to come. Wow. What a sweet man and a sweet message. Probably one of the sweetest things anyone has ever said to me in my lifetime. But I don't feel as affected as I should. Maybe I am just upset about Dad. Maybe I should at least go talk to Jeremy. It's only the 10th so he should still be in LA.

I have got to eat first. I haven't eaten since lunch yesterday with Mom.

So, after scarfing down a yogurt, I decide it's time to face this with Jeremy. He might just be the man I was meant to be with forever. I could at least give him a chance right?

I walk to the front door of my apartment and open it with keys in hand. As I look up into the most handsome blue eyes I have ever seen I know that my previous thought was completely off mark. This is the man I was supposed to spend my forever with. This one standing on my doorstep in LA. Not in Colvin, OK. Wait, in LA? Aiden is on my doorstep in LA? I must be dreaming. If this is a dream don't wake me up.

****

"Hi Karlie Mae. You look shocked to see me." I say smiling because I am so happy to see her.

"Wha- what are you doing here Aiden? I just got home a little while ago from Colvin." I don't remember her ever stuttering so I must have really surprised her. And the look on her face is priceless.

"Can we talk? I think it's way overdue." I say gesturing inside. She steps aside and lets me in a little reluctantly.

"Of course, would you like something to drink? Not sure what I have after being gone so long but I can sure look or run and get us something down the street if you want." She says rambling on. Yep I surprised her socks off. Good. She will know I mean business.

"Were you going anywhere important?"

"No, not really." I see her say knowing it is a little bit of a guilty look but I don't care. We have got to talk this out this time.

"Okay then, sit down." I motion for her to sit beside me on the couch. "I flew all the way here to clear up a little misunderstanding we had last night."

"What misunderstanding are you talking about?"

"I was at Tracey's when you went by."

"Yes, I was headed to find you. But you chose Tracey. So I left Colvin. Nothing there for me anymore." She says wiping tears from her eyes and looking away from me.

"That's where the misunderstanding started. I was at Tracey's breaking it off with her Karlie. I love you with all of my being and always have. I want to be with you forever." I say taking her hand in mine and feeling her tremble.

I kiss the back of her hand and she still hasn't said a word. Maybe I am wrong about her feelings. Could I really be that wrong? I just flew all the way to LA to profess my love for a woman who once again doesn't want me.

"Say something Karlie. Please." I plead almost scared to hear her answer. As I proceed to let go of her hand she squeezes it harder.

"Aiden I love you too. I have loved you my whole life and always will. I was so hurt that I left knowing I couldn't do it again. When I left you eight years ago I left part of my heart there in Colvin with you. I didn't realize that until I went back and saw you again." She says tears filling her eyes but with the most beautiful smile I have ever seen.

"Karlie Mae you are the best part of me." I say getting down on one knee in front of her. "You are the piece that makes my life whole and makes me who I am. Will you continue to be that piece and be my wife and love me forever?"

"Yes Aiden yes!! I want nothing more than to spend the rest of my life as your missing piece because you are that same piece for me." She says getting down on her knees in front of me too and throwing her arms around me and squealing.

"Well then it's settled! But first I have something I have wanted to do for over eight years." I say taking her in my arms and wrapping her hair around my fingers. I press my lips against hers and feel the world right itself. She lets out a little whimper and I know this was meant to be forever. As I carry her into the bedroom I look down at the woman in my arms knowing that she will forever be mine and no one else's. I know that this is what was missing and know now that I will forever be whole.

13

Looking over at a sleeping Aiden I feel like I am whole. Finally. I just need to tell Gerry. That ought to be a fun thing to do. I talked to Mom last night and she says the space above the store is perfect for KAB and will have it all cleaned out before I get home. Which I don't doubt. Something for her to do to keep herself busy. It feels as if that's what I am supposed to do now. The next step for me and my career. It may not be Fiji or London, but wherever Aiden is I will be more than happy to be.

"Where are you going?" I hear him come up behind me as I pour a cup of coffee. I have gotten dressed and am trying to be quiet and not wake him.

"I need to go talk to Gerry and break the news to him that I'm relocating to Colvin and not doing the Fiji shoot." I say waiting to see Aiden's reaction.

"I was so hoping you would want to do that. This long distance thing was going to kill me." He says with a big smile and kisses me while wrapping me in his arms.

"Aiden, I really need to go. If we are ever going to get things done and go back to Oklahoma, I need to get started. I will go talk to Gerry. Do you want to go too or what do you want to do?"

"I'll start packing things up here if that's ok." He says and steals my cup taking a big swig.

"That's fine. I should be back in a couple of hours. There is a packing store around the corner if you want to go get boxes. Or just call a moving company and they can do it for you. I don't care either way." I kiss him again and head for the door. I turn to make sure this is real. Aiden is really in my apartment in LA. And with nothing on but pajama bottoms. Good thing I called Gerry already and he's expecting me or I wouldn't be anywhere but in bed. With Aiden. That makes a grin cross my lips that seems to be a common occurrence these days.

****

"Gerry, I know it's not what you would want for me, but it's what I want and need. I love Aiden and I actually fell in love with my home town while I was there too. Look at these pictures I have been taking." I hand him a folder full of the photos I had taken in the town square and at the fundraiser.

"Wow Karlie! These are great. You might be onto something here. So, no more location shoots? Really? I thought you wanted to be a big photographer all over the world?"

"I used to be that person yes. You can still call me with opportunities but don't expect me to drop it all and run. I don't want to lose that easy spirit I had before while gallivanting around the world, but I do want to settle down.

And marry Aiden." I say smiling and playing with the newly placed ring on my left hand.

"You look and sound so different Karlie. I really am happy for you. I hope you know what you are doing. This is going to kill your professional side but just might help your personal side flourish. Good luck sweetie." He says and gives me a hug. "You need to get going and get your stuff packed up I am sure."

"Aiden is home doing that. Do you know of a good moving company? I still need to get to KAB and pack things up there too. I think I should hire someone for my personal stuff and do KAB myself. A lot of memories there that I need to deal with. Thanks Gerry, when you feel like a quiet vacation, come to Oklahoma!" I say and hug him one more time before walking out the door. Maybe for the last time. I really don't feel upset about it like I thought I would. I feel at peace.

****

"Well, this is it! This is KAB! I fell in love with the exposed brick on this wall and the modern ceiling to floor windows on this wall. What do you think?" I say with all the excitement I did the first time I saw the space.

"It's gorgeous Karlie. Are you sure you want to let it go?" he asks letting go of my hand to walk to the windows. "This view is amazing."

"Yes, the view is amazing, but it's not what I need or want anymore. If I could do this to the space above Mom's store, I would be perfectly happy. And you will be there. You aren't here." I say wrapping my arms around his neck and pulling him down for a steamy kiss that will definitely show him how serious I am about this move.

"Ok, well I'm going to start taking the furniture apart in the back. You start putting the artwork and photos away. We can knock this out in no time." And he walks away smiling. He no longer questions my decision. I think he is even whistling.

****

Karlie is in the front packing up her favorite place in LA while I am in back taking apart furniture. This seems surreal. I get to take her back to Colvin for good. As my fiancé. Will she be happy there? Will it be enough for her? That gives me a great idea so I dial Austin.

"Austin, can you call Aaron and have him go look at the space above Ella Mae's store? Karlie wants to open up her studio in there. We are packing up her LA one right now and I see how much she loves it. I want to make the one there look just like this. I will send you pictures later so that you can get them to Aaron. His company would be perfect for the renovations with the upscale stuff they do. Thanks."

I think I hear someone talking to Karlie as I hang up with Austin. I can't help but smile at the thought of how surprised she will be when the space is done.

Wait, that voice sounds familiar. But I don't know anyone here. Oh no, I remember who. Jeremy. What is he doing here? Do I stay back here or go up there and stake my claim like a caveman? Caveman it is.

****

Packing up the last big print off the wall, I look up to see Jeremy walking through the front door. Just like he used to with keys in hand. Crap. I forgot he had a key.

"Jeremy, hi. What are you doing here?"

"I heard from Dad that you were terminating your lease. You do know it's going to cost you quite a bit don't you? You leased it for another 18 months." He says walking towards me.

"Yes. I don't expect any special treatment. I already sent a check over to him for the difference." I say not knowing what to do or say in this situation. Aiden is in the back and Jeremy is up here standing in front of me. How much more awkward can this get?

"Karlie I got all of it done except the big armoire in the far back. Oh I'm sorry I didn't know you had company." He says and looks at Jeremy then back at me.

"Aiden, you remember Jeremy? He stopped by to talk to me about the lease. His Dad and their company own the building." I say stumbling with the words not really knowing what else to say.

"Nice to meet you again. I'm going to go down the street and get us some lunch. Give you guys a few minutes alone." He says and kisses my temple and walks out the door without a glance back.

"Looks like you are happy. I take it he is the one you haven't been able to get over all these years? I thought there was something there when we met in the café that day. And by the size of that rock on your hand, you are where you need to be."

"Jeremy, I never meant to rub your nose in any of this. I was actually hoping to get in and out before you were aware I was here or that I was even leaving. I never meant to hurt you. You do know that right?" I ask truly hoping he knew that.

"I know. You can't help who you love. Or who you don't." With that he walks away. That will most likely be the last time I see him. I just pray he will be happy one day.

Still standing in the same place as I was before, Aiden walks back in the front door and smiles. "You okay? That had to be tough."

"Actually, I am good. I needed to close that chapter even though I never intended to have to do it." Taking the bag from his hands and turning to walk to the only table left standing. "I'm sorry you had to deal with it."

"I could have stayed back there but knew it was him so I wanted him to know he couldn't give you a hard time. It was tough I won't lie, walking out that door leaving you with him. But, I know you love me and not him." He says winking at me and smiling.

"I do love you. What did you get us to eat? I am starved!" I say and dig into the bag not wanting to ever have this conversation again.

****

"Hey Aaron. How's the studio coming? We are about ready to head out on the road. Yeah. We'll stop in Vegas and then who knows where else. No, no Elvis wedding don't worry. Both our mothers would kill us. We should be home in a few days. Will the space be done? Oh that's good to hear. She is going to love it. I appreciate you taking time to do this for me. And Karlie. Let me know what I owe you. Thanks again."

Hanging up from the phone call with Aaron I can't help but smile knowing how much Karlie is going to love the studio. I can't wait to show it to her. I can't wait to get her home to the ranch either. I can't wait to just live my life with Karlie after wanting her all these years. And she is going to be my wife.

****

After hours of packing up and moving the boxes out to a moving van, we have my entire studio cleared out. I walk in the door and stand in the empty space and feel how unfamiliar it all seems now. I remember walking into it years ago when I first looked at it, but I was a different person back then. At the time I never expected to start dating the landlord's son either. I never expected to be changed so drastically when my father passed away. Especially never expected to find Aiden again.

Just as my thoughts drifted to Aiden, I could feel him put his hands on my shoulders pulling me back against him. He leans down and kisses my temple and at that exact Moment I know all is right with the world. I ran away from him and Colvin but was only using LA as a band aid. I really should have gone back to Colvin long before now, I know that.

"Ready to go babe?" he says and wraps his arms around me. "If we start now, we might make it to Las Vegas before dark."

"I can't believe we are driving that U-Haul all the way to Oklahoma from here. With my car on a trailer? We must be crazy." I smile and lock the door for the last time and drop the keys through the mail slot. I feel as if I am actually closing that chapter of my life and starting a new one with Aiden.

14

After a week of taking care of all things LA and driving back to Oklahoma, Aiden is about to pull into the AK Ranch but stops and points at the sign. He turns to Karlie and says, "Do you know what the AK stands for?"

She smiles and says, "No."

"Aiden Karlie." I say to her with a big smile and lean over to kiss her. "You're the ranch's missing piece too Karlie."

"Aiden!! I never knew the name of your ranch or what it meant! I love it!" She says exclaiming and throwing herself into my arms. "You do know what my photography business is named don't you?"

I shake my head no but smile. "It's something about a cab right? Isn't that what the sign said outside your LA office?"

"It's K.A.B. Photos Aiden. Karlie. Aiden. Blake. ... Get it?" She says smiling with all the love in her heart and gives me the longest and most passionate kiss I have ever had.

"Oh Karlie....." Is all I can say as we pull into the AK Ranch together. Finally.

"Looks like we have company" Karlie says as we come closer to the house.

"It's the whole family Karlie!" I say with a big smile loving the sight of my family and her mother standing on the front porch as we drive in. "They must be here to welcome you home."

"Home. That sounds wonderful Aiden!" she says with a little sigh and a big smile. Her green eyes are sparkling with tears that she is holding back.

"Hey guys, what are you all doing here?" I say as I step out of the pickup. "We weren't expecting any company."

"We are so happy to see you though!!" Karlie says slapping me on the arm before she runs off to hug her Mom and the rest of the guests.

"We have a surprise for you Karlie." Ella Mae says smiling after hugging Karlie and accepting one from me.

"A surprise? Only for Karlie?" I say smiling mischievously. "What about me?"

"Yes, it's mainly for Karlie, but I am sure you will like it too." I hear my Mom say as she steps towards me for a hug too.

After hugging everyone and finally getting inside the house we head towards the backyard. Nearing the sliding glass doors, we can see an unfamiliar man standing next to the creek.

As we get the doors open I quickly realize it's Karlie's older brother Jonathan. He must have finally made it home from Iraq. I see Karlie begin to register who the stranger is and suck in a quick breath before running off squealing to the man. She jumps into his arms and wraps hers around him just as tight as he is holding her.

I just stand there smiling knowing that everything is perfect. My heart couldn't feel happier or fuller of love.

****

As we open the doors to the patio out back I see a man standing by the creek. Before I can realize who it is he turns around and I see the face I have been longing to see since long before Dad died.

"Jonathan!!" I say squealing and running towards my older brother. "You are back!"

"Hey little sis, I guess you're surprised to see me huh?"
He says as he swings me around in his arms. "I missed
you!"

"Oh I have missed you so much Jonathan!!" I say and
hold onto him tightly. He feels so strong and mature after
being away to the war zone in Iraq. There hasn't been a day
that has gone by that I haven't been worried about him.

And now he is back and standing in front of me. Alive.
"Are you back for good?"

"Only a couple days then I get deployed back next week.
I just came home for a few days once I got all of your
messages. I am so sorry I wasn't here for you two when Dad
died." He says with a frown knowing how hard it had to
have been here.

"Well we are very happy to have you back even if it's
for a couple of days!" I say hugging my brother again. I am
trying not to get upset knowing he is going back to Iraq.

"I am very happy to be back and to see you so happy. I take it Aiden is to blame for that smile and that rock?" he says grinning from ear to ear and looks at Aiden.

"He is part of it." I say with a mischievous grin. "You definitely are the cherry on top!"

"So, when's dinner? I am starving!" he says loud enough for Mom to hear and makes everyone chuckle.

"Let's go back to our house and we can whip something up. I doubt Aiden and Karlie have much in their fridge or cupboards with the time away getting her packed up and moved home." Says Amelia as we all head inside again.

We all agree and head to our vehicles to drive to the 6AB Ranch. As a family. A family meant to be. A family that is whole at last.

****

"Thanks for agreeing to come here with me today, Jonathan." I say and loop my arm through his. "This is a special place that I wanted to share with you."

"I'm glad you asked. I was trying to find a place where I could say good-bye to Dad. I can't believe I didn't know about his passing until yesterday. I feel so guilty for not being here Karlie." Jonathan says and squeezes my arm a little tighter.

"We all knew you were overseas doing whatever it is you do. We weren't upset you weren't here because you chose not to, we knew you couldn't. We would have loved to have had you here, but understood. I am just so sorry you couldn't be here to bury him or say good-bye."

"What do you want to do about 6AB Breeds? Do you want to keep the ownership or sell it to the Blakes?"

"I would like to keep it and maybe come back after my next tour is over and take it over like Dad did."

"That's fine with me. I will go tell Aiden and he can let AJ know." By now we have reached the creek bank where I know he will feel Dad's presence.

I look up at Jonathan and say, "Do you want company or to be here alone? I'll be happy either way."

"I think I would like a little time alone, if you are sure you don't mind." He says fighting back the tears. "Are you sure Aiden doesn't mind if I am out here?"

"It was his idea to bring you down here. He fully understands that this is the one place that I feel Dad and can come to be close to him. He wants you to be able to share that too. Just come up to the house when you are done and we will have a drink. I love you Jonathan." I say and walk away fighting back my own tears. I just feel so bad that he hasn't been able to grieve for Dad the way that Mom and I have.

****

The next day I put one of my ties over Karlie's eyes and lead her to the garage and into the pickup. "Just sit here and wait and see. Relax." I am so excited to show her the studio. Aaron and his crew finished it late last night and it's all ready for Karlie to see.

"Aiden, where are we going and why do I have a blind fold on? What are you up to?" she asks with a hint of the sassy woman I fell in love with. She is too curious to be too sassy with me.

"I have a surprise for you." I say and make sure her blindfold is still in place.

We pull up behind the store in town and I get her out ready to show her the studio. I walk her around to the front so that she doesn't know where she is. I turn her to where she is facing the big sign that says KAB PHOTOS in black letters on a silver glittery background. I hope she likes it.

I take off the blindfold and she looks up blinking trying to adjust to the difference in lighting.

"OH MY GOODNESS AIDEN!!!" she says turning quickly and jumping into my arms. "You got me a sign for KAB! I LOVE IT!!"

I see Aaron open the door upstairs and hear him say, "There's more than that to see Karlie."

As he starts to speak Karlie turns to find him and I point up towards the top of the stairs.

Aiden, what did you do?" she asks with question written all over her face. I have shocked her again I can see.

"Go on up and see. I'm right behind you."

Walking up the stairs on shaky legs she reaches the top and sees through the glass door that also has KAB PHOTOS on it and begins to cry. "Oh, Aiden!" I gently push her through the door that Aaron was still holding open.

Fully inside the studio, she is clearly shaken up. It does look amazing and just like her LA studio. Even the brick wall facing the wall full of windows, dark hard wood floors and white walls covered in her work. Down to the same light fixtures she had there, it's a perfect replica. It's amazing how well Aaron matched the pictures I sent him.

"Do you like it?" I ask really hoping she was just shocked and not upset.

She hasn't said anything for a few seconds and I am starting to worry that I have overstepped. I look at Aaron and he is clearly as uncomfortable as I am. Karlie walks to the brick wall and runs her hand along the mortar between the bricks. She turns and I can see that she has tears rolling down her cheeks.

"Karlie, I didn't mean to upset you. I thought you would love this. I don't know what to say." I start walking towards her not really knowing what else to say or do. I feel as though I made a huge mistake and that she might run away again.

****

I can't believe what Aiden has done. This place looks nothing like I remember when Mom had all her junk stored up here all these years. It looks exactly like my LA studio did. The view of Colvin is the only difference. I am just stunned. It's amazing and I don't have any idea what to say. I look at Aiden and see Aaron escaping out the door in haste.

"Aiden, I don't know what to say. I am so surprised and so very touched. It looks just like my LA studio. I can't believe you guys have done all of this in such a short time. This is just amazing. Thank you so much."

"You really scared me there Karlie. I thought you were mad. I think Aaron did too as you saw him chicken out and leave as quickly as he could." I say with a snicker visualizing him as a dog with his tail between his legs.

"No, Aiden. I love it so much! I am just so touched I don't know what to say or do first. I never in a million years expected this!"

"Karlie, I love you so much. I am so very thankful you're here in Colvin with me now. I just wanted you to have the best of both worlds. Your studio was so important to you in LA so Aaron and I collaborated to make sure it was exactly the same. He did an amazing job. I know why he is so busy now." He says and starts to unbutton my top smiling that wicked Aiden smile that melts me on the spot.

"What about the door?" I ask afraid someone might come in and see us. I start to get up to lock it and pull the blind but see that the blind is down.

I look at Aiden and he looks back from the door thinking the same thing I am, "I think Aaron took care of it all. You're all mine."

"Always." I say and show Aiden just how I feel about him and his surprise studio remodel.

15

Several weeks later, I am finally all settled into the AK and back into Colvin. It has been so wonderful being a part of Aiden's life and family again. Wedding plans are in full swing and we have about two months left before the big day. Audrey, my Mom and Amelia have really been such a big help with all of these plans. Without them I don't think I could be pulling off this wedding so quickly. A three month engagement isn't long for normal couples, but Aiden and I are far from normal. It's almost like it has been in the making for over eight years, so what is another three months, right?

"Aiden, Jonathan and I discussed the ownership of 6AB Breeds and we have decided to keep it. He wants to be able to come back here after his next tour is over and take it over like Dad used to. Do you think that would be ok?"

"That would be perfect. Dad will actually be very happy to hear that."

"Aiden, what color do you want your tuxes to be? Tie or bowtie?" I ask while trying to nail down a list of details Audrey told me to decide on today. "We need to get all of the color stuff finalized."

"Um, black tux like James Bond." Aiden says and laughs. "Seriously though, black tux with black bowtie. Classic."

"Sounds sexy. Thank you." I say standing up and kissing him before walking away to call Audrey with those details.

"Audrey, he wants a black tux and black bowtie. The classic. Nope. He says like James Bond. There will be enough silver and cream other places, his tux isn't going to throw it off don't worry. Thanks Audrey!"

I think I need some time alone to clear my head so I head to the barn to saddle up Spook.

Fully engrossed in the job at hand I don't hear Aiden until he speaks from directly behind me. "You want company?"

"Nah. Audrey is stressing me out with all the wedding stuff and I want to go clear my head. I'll be back later." I kiss him and swing up into the saddle. Aiden just nods and walks away. I'm sure he is headed back to the house and to the office.

****

Knock. Knock.

I hear the knocking and look up expecting to see Karlie but its Tracey. At first I don't think much of it but then it hits me. She just came inside the house without ringing the doorbell like she used to. It's a darn good thing Karlie isn't here, she would have a fit.

"Tracey, what are you doing here?" I ask feeling a little bit annoyed. "I didn't hear the doorbell."

"I didn't use it." She says as if nothing were wrong with that.

"Um, you don't live here and we aren't together, so you really need to use it from now on."

"Well, good thing Karlie is gone then."

"Tracey, what do you want?" I ask this time not trying to hide my annoyance with her.

Knowing I am trying to usher her to the front door she stops and says, "We need to talk Aiden."

"We don't have anything to talk about. So, why are you really here?" I can't help but let my feelings known in the tone of my voice. "I don't have time for this and Karlie should be back anytime."

"Well, you might want to make time for this. I'm pregnant with your child Aiden." She says with a smile on her face that should have been a good thing.

"YOU'RE WHAT?" I scream a little too loud.

"We are going to have a baby Aiden! Aren't you excited? I am so excited!!" she says and tries to wrap her arms around me.

I keep her from doing so and back away a few steps from her and say, "How long have you known? Are you sure?"

"Yes Aiden, I am sure. The little positive sign is hard to misread. I just found out this morning."

"Um. Um. I'm not sure what to say Tracey. We haven't been together in so long. I never expected this. And Karlie. What is she going to say? We are planning a wedding!" with those realizations I start to feel light headed and ready to pass out. Walking back into my office and sitting down allows Tracey time to touch my arm in concern which makes me recoil. That feels wrong. Very wrong.

"Well, I will go and let you know when my first doctor's appointment is so you can go with me. Good luck with Karlie. Talk to you later!" she says and leaves me shocked and quite a bit freaked out.

****

After regaining my composure, I drive over to the 6AB hoping to find my sister there. She is Tracey's best friend so she will know what I am supposed to do and if this is even real.

Walking into the kitchen I ask, "Audrey, have you talked to Tracey today?"

"No. Why? Something wrong?" she asks unsure of what's going on. "You look like you are going to pass out."

"She just came to the house and let herself in like she used to. I was in the office and she came back there. She acted like we never broke up and um…." I say not wanting to say those words.

"Aiden, what is going on? You're scaring me!"

"She said she is pregnant." I say before finally collapsing onto the bar stool at the kitchen island unable to keep myself upright.

"Oh my gosh Aiden! I didn't know! When did she find out?" she squeals and grabs my hands from across the countertop. "Wow, no wonder you are white as a ghost. What did Karlie say?"

"She is out on a ride in the north pasture. Tracey seemed to know she wasn't there too." I slowly say knowing this is going to break Karlie's heart.

"What are you going to do brother? How are you going to tell her? It's going to kill her. She's already uneasy about Tracey." I want to bang my head on that countertop.

"I promised her it was over with Tracey and she wasn't even a part of my life anymore. How do I tell her that isn't so true anymore?" I sigh and say shaking my head. My worst fear has just come true. I was with Tracey for over three years and this never happened but once I finally get Karlie and she agrees to marry me this happens. What am I going to tell her?

"Aiden, you didn't plan this baby. You're going to have to tell Karlie and pray she understands exactly that. I have a ton of lessons plans to do in my classroom so I have to go. Love you brother. I'm here if you need me. I will talk to Tracey too." She gives my shoulder a squeeze and heads for the door. I am once again left alone freaked out.

****

"Hey baby, I'm back. Gonna shower, then we need to go to town and help Mom figure out if her yard will work for the ceremony and reception." I say walking into Aiden's office. It helps having the ranch office in the house because when I need to talk to him, he is close by.

"Ok. I'll be ready when you are." Aiden says looking a bit out of sorts. He must be engrossed in something important for the ranch.

I walk to our room and bathroom. Once there I undress and shower thinking about how I really do envision Mom's backyard. I hope we can make it work there. It would mean the world to me to get married in the yard I played in since I could walk and a yard where my father worked so hard to make perfect for my Mom. And I know Mom wants us to have it there. She always tells us that she and Dad had my wedding in mind when they re-did it years ago when I left home.

Austin is meeting us there too so he can get a feel for the flowers since he works at Stampley's Nursery. He does such an amazing thing with flowers and they grow gorgeous ones too. It was a no brainer who our wedding florist would be. Is he even called a florist? Who knows? Flower person. Whatever.

That makes me chuckle and I finish my shower and towel off. Wrapping myself in a towel, I go to the bedroom doorway and yell at Aiden, "Hey! We have a little time if you want to do something else!" I smile and wait for his response.

"I'm still trying to get this last column to balance. I'll be there in a minute." I hear him say from down the hall.

That's weird; he has never turned me down before. Come to think of it, he would never have let me shower alone either! Something is definitely bothering him today. He has been off since I got back from my ride. Hmmm. Hope all is ok with the ranch books.

Knowing he won't be joining me, I get dressed and ready to go to town.

****

Karlie has to know something is wrong. On a normal day I would never let her shower alone or turn her down to make love to her especially in the middle of a Saturday. I just can't get Tracey's words out of my head. And I can't stop wondering how in the world do I break the news to my fiancé? Heck when it's born she will be my wife. If she still wants to marry me after I do tell her. I think that's what I am most worried about.

I hear Karlie coming down the hall so I close down my computer and follow her to the front door. We are going to pick out flowers and the location for the wedding and here I am not sure if there even will be one. It will crush me if she does cancel it.

"Ready? Austin is meeting us there in 30 minutes. Mom is already there with Reverend Lowell." She says smiling that excited smile. She is so excited about the wedding, how can I destroy all that with the news that will break her heart? What choice do I have though? This is a small town, she will find out regardless.

****

"Mom, this will be perfect. Don't you think baby?" I say hugging Mom and then Aiden. "The cream colored assortment of flowers will be my first choice Austin. Thanks for coming over here to meet us. I'm sure you were busy at the nursery. We really appreciate it."

"Yes, thanks Austin. Jack left the best person in charge. You picked great stuff." Aiden says not really sounding excited as he was earlier today. The tux decision must have been his last one. That's ok. With Audrey, Amelia, Mom and I, we are sure to get it all done in perfect time. No problem.

I walk over to Aiden and wrap my arms around his waist and lay my head on his chest. I hear his heart beating strong and I feel more happy and content than I have ever felt. But I can't help but wonder what is up with him and his mood.

"What happened while I was out riding? The ranch books ok?" I feel him breathe in deep and let out a big sigh. "Aiden?"

"Nothing baby. Just ranch stuff. I don't mean to put a damper on the wedding details; I just have a lot on my mind." He says and kisses the top of my head.

Stepping out of his arms and raising on my tip toes to kiss his lips, I lightly say, "Ok, if you say so. I need to run to Mom's store and see if I can find the wedding cake books so we can finalize the design tonight too. I will get a ride back with Audrey. Love you."

Walking away I feel as if he isn't telling me something but I have more to worry about than what Aiden's embarrassed to tell me about ranch finances. Mom's paying for the wedding so, it doesn't directly relate to me.

"Hey Audrey. Can you drop me off at the AK on your way home? Aiden had a lot going on at the ranch so he left me at Moms." I call her and ask. Luckily I knew she was at the school in her classroom this afternoon working on lesson plans.

I walk to Mom's store and just before I walk into it I get a text.

Love you.

From Aiden. I type a quick reply and hit send and receive another right away.

Promise?

What does that mean? What a weirdo. I text back.

Always. You?

Knowing what his answer will be I search for books and when I find them I head back to Moms. As I lock up the store, my phone chimes again.

No doubt.

Ok maybe he is just stressed out with the ranch today. Before I get a block away from the store I see Tracey drive by slowly and wave like she's my best friend. I smile and wave back hesitantly. Now that was bizarre. I haven't really seen or talked to her since we got back from LA. Weird. Everyone is acting strange today. Something in the air?

****

After about an hour of looking at the wedding cake books with Mom, I hear Audrey call out from the front door. I yell back and tell Mom I have to go. Give her a kiss on the cheek and carry the books and my purse to meet Audrey at her car.

"Hey. Thanks for the ride. Aiden was so distracted earlier. We did decide on flowers with Austin and to for sure have the wedding and reception in Mom's back yard."

She smiles a hesitant smile and says, "I'm sure it will be magical."

Now Audrey is taking the crazy train ride too. She is usually going non-stop with wedding details.

"The strangest thing happened today when I was walking back from the store to Moms. I saw Tracey drive by slowly and waved like a crazy person. So strange." I say knowing Audrey and Tracey were close. If something was wrong, she would know.

"That is strange. She didn't say anything? Just waved?" she asks without taking her eyes off the road.

"No. Just waved. I waved and smiled or at least tried to but it was just eerie." I say with a big sigh thinking I need to just relax because I am getting paranoid and sounding like I am the one on the crazy train ride.

Once we pull up in front of my house at the AK, I look over at Audrey and say, "Thanks for the ride. Talk soon."

She pulls away a little faster than normal and I am left standing in my driveway shaking my head. Seriously, what is up with everyone today?

****

After texting Karlie I feel even worse than before. I am keeping something so monumental from her and don't know what to do. Well, I know what to do. I need to tell her, but I can't make those words come out of my mouth.

Just then my phone rings, "Hi Audrey. What's up? SHE WHAT? Did she say anything to her? I know I just don't know what to say. She was so pumped for wedding stuff. How in one breath do I tell her yes I love the white flowers versus the pink then the next tell her another woman is pregnant with my first child? I know Audrey, I will soon. Thanks. Night."

"You will what?" I hear Karlie come into the kitchen and say. Oh goodness how much did she just hear?

"I will ask Austin to be my best man." I lie and reach for her wrapping my arms around her knowing this could be one of the last times I get to do this.

"I think I am going to ask Audrey to be my maid of honor. What do you think?" she asks.

"Great. She's acting more like the wedding planner than maid of honor anyway." I say with a smile at the thought of my little sister bossing everyone around.

"She's been such a big help. I couldn't be pulling off this wedding in three months without her. And our mothers, of course." She says and gives me a saucy look and pulls me towards the bedroom. This time I definitely won't be turning her down. The news will have to come later.

After I tell her the news, she may not want to be this close to me again. I hope she doesn't pick up on my desperation. I can't imagine going back to not being able to kiss, touch or make love to her whenever I feel like it. But it seems inevitable.

16

A couple days later I am in my studio for some appointments I have and find Tracey walking in the front door instead of my client. She is holding her stomach like she is ill. If she's ill why is she in here? I don't want to get sick. Seeing her twice in one week is two too many. What is she doing here? I don't hate her; it's just too weird being around her.

"Hello. What can I do for you?" I ask politely.

"Don't we need to talk about it? I thought I would have heard from you by now." She says with more attitude than necessary. That has never been the way she has acted before. But what is she talking about anyway? I have nothing to talk to her about. She is acting so strange.

"Talk about what? Why would I call you?" I say starting to feel uncomfortable. I look at my watch to check the time hoping it was time for my next client to arrive, but no luck. Still have a few minutes.

"He didn't tell you did he? He told Audrey but not his beloved Karlie?" she spits out and steps a bit closer as if ready to do battle.

"Just get it out Tracey, what do you want? I have clients coming any minute and don't have time for your games." I say tiring of this nonsense. As I say that the front door rips open and Aiden rushes in clearly mad at someone. And on the war path.

****

"Aiden, I just talked to Tracey and she said she was going to KAB to talk to Karlie. She doesn't know you haven't told her yet. You better hurry up and diffuse the situation before world war three starts in the middle of that studio." I hear Audrey say on the other side of the phone call. I hang up quickly in full panic, jump in my pickup and race into town praying I can catch Tracey before she says anything to Karlie. Darn it! Why haven't I just manned up and told her already? I was afraid this was going to happen.

If Tracey tells Karlie first, I'm a dead man. I have to get there before so I can tell her myself. Tracey won't use any tenderness at all and Karlie is going to be so upset.

Finally pulling up in front of KAB, I see that Tracey is here. Oh crap! I race up the steps and rip open the door. The women are standing in the middle of the room looking as if they are ready to go a few rounds.

Karlie looks at me with so much confusion I can tell that Tracey wasn't able to say anything yet. I couldn't be any luckier than that.

"Tracey, can I have a few minutes alone with Karlie, please?" I ask pleading with the woman I used to think I loved.

"Sure, why not? I have a doctor's appointment in a few minutes anyway so I will come by later." She says with a smile and walks out the door. I know what doctor she is seeing but I feel nothing about not being with her for it. Right now, Karlie is my first priority.

"What is going on here Aiden?" Karlie asks as she still stands there looking confused. "She was acting so strange."

"Baby, you need to sit down. I need to tell you something." I say grabbing her hands and sitting in front of her. "You aren't going to like what I have to say."

"Aiden, please don't tell me she is pregnant!" she screams and pulls away from me as she puts all the pieces to the puzzle together. Smart was always something Karlie was.

"Baby, I just found out a couple of days ago. I have been trying to find the right time and the right way to tell you." I stand and walk to the window running my hands through my hair.

"A couple of days? You have been keeping something like this from me all this time? How could you Aiden? This affects my life too! I can't believe this! Now it all seems clear. The way you have been acting. Audrey all weird. Tracey. Oh my gosh. This can't be happening. How can this be happening Aiden?" she says and begins to cry but steps back as I try to step towards her. She holds up her hand to gesture me to stop.

"She says she just found out earlier this week. I am so sorry Karlie. Please tell me what to say." I plead with the love of my life as I feel her slipping away from me.

"Don't know what to say? You slept with her and she got pregnant Aiden. Not much you can say! How far along is she? We have been together almost two months. Have you been sleeping with her since we got back? How would you feel if I told you I was pregnant with Jeremy's baby right now? Yes, just like that." she squeaks out and puts her hand over her mouth.

"No Karlie! I would never do that. I love you more than anything! It has to be from before we broke up. I was always so careful with her. For over three years. Oh Karlie, please tell me you understand this isn't something I wanted." I say and wipe tears from my eyes as well as see Karlie wiping more than a few from hers.

"Please leave Aiden. You should be at that doctor's appointment anyway. You are the father." With that she lets a slight sob escape and turns to run to the back room of the studio leaving me standing here frozen. Again feeling as if my life were a nightmare.

****

"Audrey, I got there right before Tracey said anything. Yes, I told her. How do you think it went? She told me to leave. No. She doesn't want to see me. Yes, she is mad I didn't tell her then. I know. I know. I really messed up. How is this happening?" I say into the phone and wish I could just wake up a few days ago and find this has never happened.

I get into my pickup and head to the hospital. Karlie is right; I should at least be there for the baby. I drive over to the side that is the clinic but don't see Tracey's car so I dial her number.

"Tracey, I am here at the clinic and I don't see your car. Where are you parked?"

"Oh I already went in and am back home. They just wanted to do the blood test to be sure before anything else was done. I am too early in the pregnancy to need much else. My next one is next month." I hear her say and wonder what the heck she is talking about. I don't know much about babies but I do know that she has to be over three months along and a doctor has to want to do more right? Hmmm. I need to ask Mom.

Mom. Oh my. That's another person I have to tell. Lightning strike me now.

I hang up my phone and head to the 6AB so I can break the not so wonderful news to my parents. I hope they take it a little better than Karlie did. But how did I expect her to take it? We are getting married in less than a month and now I am an expectant father. With another woman.

I take a deep breath and walk into the kitchen where Mom and Dad are with Audrey and Austin. The whole gang's here and I get to tell them news that will alter everything. Oh boy.

Everyone looks my way as I walk into the room. From the looks on their faces I can tell that Audrey has already broke the news to them. Not sure if I am relieved or mad. Mom walks over and hugs me tight. Well, she isn't too mad if she wants to hug me. The rest of them follow and I feel as if my dog just died.

"So, Audrey spilled the beans I take it?" I ask trying to add a bit of humor but it falls flat. This is too serious for humor.

"Aiden, how could you not tell us? And Karlie? Son, what is going to happen now?" Mom asks while stopping to stand next to my Dad.

"I was trying to process and find the right way and time to tell Karlie. She had to know first. I'm sorry you didn't find out earlier. Very sorry. I just don't know what to do here. I never in a million years thought this would ever happen to me. And now Karlie wants nothing to do with me right now." I finally break down with what seems like the weight of the world on my heart.

****

How can this be happening? Aiden and Tracey are going to have a baby. Not he and I. I always dreamed of being the one to hand him his first born child. After we were married. Not before and with someone else having that honor. Sitting down on the sofa in KAB I start to feel like I can breathe a little better. I have got to get out of here. I can't go home. I can see if Mom is in the store or at home. Mom will know to comfort me. I have to tell her first. If I tell Mom it will be real.

"Mom, I need to talk to you. It's very important. Can you meet me at home? Good. Heading there now." I say into my cell phone and lock up the studio. I climb into my SUV and somehow drive myself the few blocks to where Mom's house is. I don't really remember driving there just like the day Dad died. I feel about the same as I did then. Except it was Aiden who hurt me this time and not the one to comfort me.

"Hi honey. What's going on? Have you been crying?" Mom asks and hugs me tightly. At that exact Moment my thoughts and emotions collide and I can't stand on my own. Mom lets me fall to the floor but never letting go of me. We sit on the floor in the hallway for a few minutes before she asks again. "What's going on Karlie? You are scaring me!"

I take a deep breath and look up at her. "Aiden is going to be a father. With Tracey." That makes me sob all over again but I hear Mom's gasp and feel her pull me tighter into the embrace. If only Mom's arms could make the hurt and the outside world go away.

"When did you find this out? You two have been together for months Karlie. How can this be?" she says with matching confusion. "Karlie, what are you going to do?"

I don't have a clue as of how to answer that. I only wished I knew what I was supposed to do or what I could be able to handle doing. I do know I don't want to deal with this. I just can't do this. I am supposed to be planning my wedding. Not figuring out how to deal with another person being a part of my marriage. Another two people.

"I need to be alone Mom. I'll be in my room." I say and escape to my old bedroom. It is even emptier this time after moving all of my stuff into the AK after LA. I sit down on my bed and feel my head swirling with all of this so I lay back. Looking up at the ceiling like I did so many nights as a child and teenager, I have never felt more at a loss. More empty inside.

****

"Karlie, are you sure this is what you should be doing? You haven't even talked to Aiden for a couple of days and you are just going to run away again? I'm not so sure about this." Mom says to me a couple mornings later as I am packing the little bit of clothes that Mom and Audrey got for me from the AK. I called Gerry last night and he has an opportunity for me in Miami to do a cover photo shoot. I told him I was taking it and would be down there today. I know Mom isn't happy but after spending a few days cooped up in my old bedroom, I need to get away from here and think.

"I will only be gone a week and a half Mom. I will be able to think a lot more clearly away from here. That bedroom of mine here feels as if the walls are closing in on me. I will stay with Savannah and get to spend time with her and the kids too. It will be much better than moping around here." I say trying very hard to sound optimistic even though that is the last thing that I am feeling.

Sleeping and waking up alone has been horrible and I severely miss Aiden, I just don't know what to say to him or what to feel. I don't know how to accept that another woman is going to be having a separate part of his life and attention. I know that sounds selfish but how can I not feel that way right now? I keep waiting for him to call me or come by but he hasn't so that must mean he is busy trying to deal with her and the baby. That will only get worse the farther along she gets and much worse after the baby is born. Their baby. Ahhhhhh.

"Ok, well I love you Karlie and will be here waiting for you to come home again. Have a safe flight." Mom says and kisses my cheek and walks out the door. A pang of guilt hits me as I realize that I am leaving her again too. I tried to get her to come with me but she used the store as her excuse again. I can't blame her. She has never lived anywhere but Colvin.

Taking a deep breath I get into my car and point it down the highway out of Colvin and towards the Tulsa airport. Where a plane is awaiting to take me out of this disaster of a situation I have here. Again.

****

"Thought you would want to know that Karlie just left for Miami. She is taking a job down there on some magazine. She should be back in ten days but with the way things are with Aiden, I wouldn't be surprised if she doesn't come back. She is really hurt Amelia. I know. He is hurting too but Karlie is the one losing in this battle, Aiden is gaining a child. One that isn't Karlie's. I'm not sure what they are going to do about the wedding, but we have to just hang on to what we have already done and just pray that before long they will work it out. Thanks, you too. Talk soon. Bye." Ella Mae hangs up the store phone and frowns knowing that Amelia feels just as helpless as she does when it comes to helping their kids work through this.

17

"Aiden, where are you?" Audrey calls out inside the

barn.

"Over here with Spook. What are you doing here?" I

ask leaning my head back against the stall wall. I am sitting

in here with my legs stretched out, ankles crossed and head

leaned back. I feel closest to Karlie in here because of the

many years we have shared around him.

"I just talked to Karlie and I thought you should know

she is in Miami. She left yesterday. She's doing a shoot

there for that guy she worked for in LA. She is staying with

Savannah but plans to be back in a little over a week. If she comes back." She says and sits down on the hay bale outside the stall.

"Are you telling me she won't be back again? Audrey, seriously?" I pipe up and sit up stock straight fully aware of the seriousness of this.

"Her plane comes back then, but whether she will or not, it's too soon to know. Have you seen Tracey since the news all hit?" she asks and tries to smile to make me feel a little better. But it doesn't. I don't like seeing anyone smile right now.

"I tried to go the other day to her doctor appointment but I guess the doctor only wanted to do the blood test to ensure she was actually pregnant. He made her an appointment next month. That's all I know." I say and wipe my hand over my face trying to wake myself up from this nightmare I am clearly having.

"They didn't even do an exam? She says she is almost four months along so he should have at least done one and probably done a sonogram. That's really weird." She says and scrunches up her forehead showing just how strange it all seemed to her. I know nothing about babies or pregnancies so I don't understand the issue.

"Well, that's what she said. I have no choice but to wait I guess. I'm sorry you are caught in the middle. I know it's tough thinking bad about your best friend. She isn't a bad girl, just didn't do the news delivery the right way."

"Well, it's all weird. A teacher from the high school just had her first sonogram and she is barely three months along. So it's strange that it's so different with Tracey. Maybe they have a different doctor. Have to go. Love you brother."

I look around and feel as though even the barn looks different without Karlie a part of it. The house has not been the same since she left. I don't sleep much, I don't eat there, and I can't get any work done there. Even when Tracey and I broke up I never felt the loss when I was in the house. Bringing Karlie here and moving her in changed the whole thing. She made the house a home instead of just a roof over our heads. But now it's empty and she is gone to Miami.

What else do I expect? This small town can gossip and I'm sure she feels embarrassed. Even more than I do because she feels like such an outsider.

I take my phone out and text her not knowing if she will even reply.

Have a good time in Miami. Be safe. Love you always.

Nope. No reply. I should have known even though I know she still loves me. Maybe it is a good idea that she went to Miami. Wish I could have gone with her.

****

Wrapping up the day of shooting in the Miami heat, I wait for the car service to pick me up and drive me back to Savannah's. I have been here for almost 24 hours and it feels great. Just not the same since I have had Aiden beside me for the past couple months. I keep catching myself trying to send him texts about what I see and what I want to do but before I can I stop myself.

As I shake off those thoughts I hear my phone chime in

my purse. Probably Savannah wondering when I will be

there. She wants to go out to dinner for a girl's night. I take

the phone out and gasp as I see who sent it and what was

sent. I can't reply. He has to know I am upset and don't

want to talk to him. But I want nothing more than to reply

that I love him always. Always. Even if he has a new

family with someone else.

I scroll through my contacts and call Savannah. "Hey

you. Yep, just got in the car and headed your way. Be there

in a few." I smile and say knowing she is running around the

house trying to get her kids ready for the babysitter. Her

husband has been in Hong Kong on business since I arrived

and I'm not so sure he will be back before my flight home.

That seems weird too because I never hear her talking to

him. The kids don't even ask where their father is. Who am

I to judge with the state of my relationship back in Colvin? I

just sit back in the seat and watch the Miami scenery change

from skyscrapers to condos and huge houses with palm trees

in the front yards.

Savannah lives in a gated community close to the ocean but it's a secluded spot that allows privacy for celebrities and families not wanting the spotlight on them when home. She even told me that she thinks a well-known comedian has a house a block over from hers and a famous basketball player a couple farther over. Not sure what Savannah's husband does, but they sure live in the lap of luxury.

Pulling up in front of her house, I get out and once again look at the front of it and it takes my breath away. It's such an immaculate place and it makes me really miss the AK. I would give anything to be back a week ago when Aiden and I made love in the big bathtub and didn't have a care in the world except for what color of flowers and ribbon to use for the wedding. The wedding. What are we going to do about the wedding? Can I go through with it knowing what I know now? Heck I don't even know if Aiden still wants to marry me or if he wants to marry Tracey to make a stable home for their baby. Marry her? Karlie come on.

I walk into Savannah's house and try to put the outside situation behind me at least for the night.

****

"So, have you talked to Aiden at all since you left?"

"No. I don't know what to say to him. It kills me to think

that she is carrying his baby. I was supposed to be the one to

give him his first child. Not her. I just don't understand

how this all could happen. Things were so good. We are so

close to the wedding. Was so close. Ugh!"

"Are you sure you don't want to still marry Aiden? You

have loved each other most of your lives."

"Loved each other? What are you talking about?"

"I have known forever, the whole town has known, that

you two were head over heels in love with each other for as

long as we can remember. Neither of you was willing to

take the chance though. Being friends was all you could

guarantee would happen between you. Am I wrong?"

"Yes, I didn't know that though until after the funeral

and Aiden found me at the creek."

"The creek at the 6AB. Boy have I ever heard about that place a million times over the years."

"It's my favorite place be nice."

"Oh I was being nice. My point is, are you sure you want to throw all of that away just because a baby was conceived while you two were with other people? You had someone else too. It could very easily have happened to you and Jeremy. Am I right?"

"I guess you're right. I hadn't thought about it that way. It hurt so much to hear that she was pregnant. I let the jealousy get the best of me a little too much. I ran away again, like I have every time a problem came up with Aiden. I am so dumb. I promised him I wouldn't run away again after he came after me in LA."

"He texted you earlier didn't he?"

"Yes, but I didn't reply. He said to have a good time here in Miami, be safe and that he loved me always."

"Aww and you want to give that up? Who cares if you have to accept another person into your fairy tale? It's real life Karlie. You of all people should know that after losing your father."

"Savannah, this was supposed to be a ladies night out without any men involved. Why did you have to bring him up? I have been trying so hard to not think about him or to miss him."

"How has that worked out for you?"

"You are evil. You know perfectly well that he is all I can think about. I could have sworn I saw him about twenty times during this week. I guess I have expected him to come after me again. I have been a little selfish haven't I?"

"A little? Just kidding. So you freaked out when you heard the news. Who can blame you? I know Aiden doesn't. When you are done with this shoot, you need to go home and talk to him. Seriously sit down and have that hard conversation. Figure out if you can make your relationship work exactly the way it is but with his child in it too."

"Ok, no more talking just more drinking. I want to have some fun! I will think about this all later when we are not dressed like this and surrounded by people like this."

"Whatever you say Karlie."

Climbing into bed tonight and the world is spinning and I don't remember ever having this much alcohol in my system. Ever. Too many margaritas. Dancing around laughing and drinking kept my mind off of Aiden and Colvin. But now that I am climbing into my bed at Savannah's house, I can't help but let my thoughts go to him. Can't help remembering lying in his arms in our bed, hearing him tell me that he loves me. Telling him that I love him just as much. Dreaming of what our wedding was going to be like and finally being able to call him my husband.

I sigh and roll over to look at the clock. It's midnight in Colvin. I can't help but wonder what Aiden is doing right now. Wonder if he misses me still or if he is moving on with Tracey and their baby. I grab my phone off the night stand

and start to send him a text but realize that he isn't mine to text anymore. May never be again.

****

"Tracey, I called to let you know that I made another appointment at the clinic so that I can be there and ask some questions. It's tomorrow at 10:15. Let me know if you need me to swing by and pick you up or if you are going to just meet me there. Thanks. Bye." I leave on her voicemail. I made the appointment more for myself than anyone because this all still doesn't seem real. Yes, Karlie left me days ago and I have been absolutely miserable without her, but the whole baby thing has left me feeling so uneasy and not like an expectant father should feel. And that isn't fair to the baby.

The next morning I still haven't heard from Tracey. I have tried several more times this morning with no call back. Oh wait, that is until now.

"Finally, I have been trying to get ahold of you since yesterday. Did you get my message?"

"Yes, Aiden, I did. I didn't ask for you to make another appointment. I have another next month and you can just wait until that one to ask your questions." And she hung up. Why is she so mad at me? I thought she wanted me to be more involved in this? I was trying to be a better person in this impossible situation and she bit my head off. I'll just go by myself then. I guess I don't really need her to be there to ask the questions anyway.

Walking into the clinic I definitely feel out of place. There are mothers with their young children and pregnant women all over the place. Maybe I shouldn't be here without Tracey. Before I can change my mind though the receptionist who happens to be a lady from our church sees me and waves me over.

"Aiden, how are you? What can I do for you?"

"I called and made an appointment for Tracey Wheeler and myself for 10:15. She decided not to come though so it's just me. I have a lot of questions for her doctor." I say feeling a bit embarrassed by the situation. I don't know if it's gone viral or not but I still feel like I am under a microscope.

"Well, I really shouldn't be telling you this, but Tracey isn't a patient here Aiden. At least not yet. I heard you two were expecting but haven't seen her in yet. Please let her know she really needs to get in for her first exam and get things started. Time flies when you least expect it to." She says and hands me a stack of pregnancy pamphlets which makes me even more uncomfortable.

I am standing here stunned. She must be able to read the shock on my face because she just smiles and asks, "Anything else you need Aiden?"

I shake my head no and turn to walk out the door. I am more confused than before about Tracey and this baby. She told me she came the other day. But that lady says no. What is going on here?

I open my pickup door and climb inside. Once in the silence and safety of the cab, I dial Tracey's number. No answer. Imagine that. I'll just swing by her house then and make her talk to me. So, I put on my seatbelt, start the pickup and drive towards her apartment building fully intent on getting to the bottom of this.

****

"Tracey, answer the door! I know you're here! Your car is outside!" I yell while beating on her door once again. The neighbors are starting to hear me and I'm able to catch them peeping out their windows to see what all the ruckus is about. "Come on Tracey!" Why isn't she answering? I never had a key to her apartment when we were together so I can't even use that. How else do I get in?

Audrey! She has a key!

"Audrey I need you to come open up Tracey's apartment. I have been beating on her door for the past ten minutes and she isn't answering. Yes, her car is here. I know she is. Yes, I'll wait here but hurry up!" Hanging up my cell phone I see George and Mable, the older couple from across the courtyard, coming up my way. Great, I bet they called the cops.

"I'm sorry for the noise. I just can't get her to answer the door." I say apologizing for how bad this whole situation must look.

"Aiden, it's ok. She is here we haven't seen her leave today. There was a lady there with her all night but she left earlier this morning. They got pretty rowdy so I bet Tracey is in bed still. What do you need?" George asks and shakes my hand. "Good to see you back around here."

"Like a party? That's not good." I exclaim needing inside even more to see what's going on. What is she thinking?

"Son, I'm sure she is ok. We didn't actually see her drinking, just carrying in some bottles of alcohol. That friend of hers has been coming around a lot since you two broke up. She may even stay several days at a time. Tracey doesn't leave her apartment much but when she does it's with that lady." Mabel says and gives her husband's arm a squeeze conveying that it is time to move on. I lean over and lightly hug each one and watch as they walk away arm in arm. A bit of my heart tugs and I can't help but wish that would be Karlie and I when we are their ages.

I try knocking a few more times with no answer so I sit on the front step to wait on Audrey. Luckily I only have to wait a few minutes before she shows up with a very worried look on her face. She quickly unlocks the door and I am relieved that I can finally go inside and figure out what is going on.

But we both stop in our tracks as we see the terrible state that her apartment is in. The place is filthy. A week's worth of fast food containers and junk food, alcohol bottles and glasses, and clothes just laying everywhere. And the smell is horrendous! Looking at Audrey beside me, she has a hand over her mouth and nose unable to grasp the site either.

"I haven't been over here in a few weeks Aiden. I call and call but she never answers or returns the calls. I honestly got wrapped up in my own life and helping with your wedding that I let her slip through. I am ashamed to say."

I put my hand on her back to comfort her and say, "It's not your fault Audrey, she is an adult. Maybe you should go check the bedrooms to see if she is in there." I step aside to allow her to move on but shake my head in disgust. How can anyone live like this?

"Aiden! Hurry!" I hear Audrey yell from the back bedroom. I rush in the door to see the worst sight yet.

Laying diagonal on the bed is a passed out female with barely any clothes on and a rubber band wrapped tightly around her upper left arm. Once it registers that it's Tracey I fly to her side to check if she is alive. She is faintly breathing and thankfully alive. I say her name a few times when she finally starts to open her eyes. Oh thank goodness. I thought she was dead when I first came in.

She sits up groggy and unaware of her surroundings. I can tell by the look on her face she is really wondering what I am doing here. She looks down at her arm and rips off the rubber band and hides it underneath her. I lift a syringe off of the floor and ask, "Looking for this?"

She takes it from my hand and tries to jump off the bed but her body isn't ready so she falls back down.

"What are you two doing here? How did you get in?" she whispers unable to look at either of us as she speaks. She is full of embarrassment and shame.

I stand up and say, "I called Audrey to come use her key. You weren't answering your door and I was worried because your car was outside. Thought maybe something was wrong with the baby. You didn't show up for the appointment this morning."

After a few minutes of silence she finally looks up at me and says, "There is no baby Aiden. I lied to get you to take me back." Tracey puts her head back down but continues, "I was at an all-time low after I heard you proposed to Karlie and I thought a baby would make you come back to me."

Almost forgetting she was in the room, I hear Audrey say from the corner, "Tracey, how long have you been doing this stuff?"

"The week I heard about the engagement. I was in Tulsa and met Barbara in a club. It helped me forget what a shamble my life was in. I just started doing more and more as the details about your wedding kept coming in. Small towns. Where is Barbara anyway?" she says and starts to walk out of the room but stumbles again causing Audrey to step forward and help steady her.

"No one else is here. Let's get you cleaned up." She takes Tracey into the bathroom while I stand here feeling like a total jerk. She has been struggling with all of this alone because I left her behind and never looked back. She didn't even cry when we broke up so I thought she was ok. I have been just as wrapped up in me and Karlie as Audrey was. Neither of us even thought about Tracey. And now look at her.

Now she is an addict and nothing like the clean freak she was before. I stand up and start cleaning the place up. That's the least I can do for her. To help remedy the problem, even if it's a slight amount of help. Walking to the

pantry I find there is no food at all in this house. None.
What has she been eating? Hence all the take out boxes.

After about 30 minutes of cleaning and several trips to
the dumpster, the ladies come out of the bedroom holding a
couple suit cases. Tracey looks a little bit more like the girl I
spent over three years of my life with but still so much like a
stranger. The sunken in face and bony structure, she does
look horrible even cleaned up.

"What's with the bags?" I ask stepping towards them
and taking them from their hands.

"I'm going to go with her to Dallas today and her
parents are going to get her into rehab there tomorrow."
Audrey says for Tracey who hasn't looked at me. She
surveys the change in the room and I know she is
embarrassed that I was the one to clean it and even see it like
it was. I should be furious with her because of the problems
the fake pregnancy caused, but with the state she is in makes
me feel so sorry for her. And quite a bit guilty.

"Do you need me to go with you? This is my fault after all." I say looking at Tracey who lifts her head and looks at me.

"No, Aiden. None of this is your fault. I had a little trouble with drugs in college but never told anyone. Not even Audrey. I let this happen. I need for you to go live your life the way it was meant to be. With Karlie. I'm so sorry about the pregnant thing. I know she left you because of it. I am just so sorry." She says and runs out the front door in tears.

"Take care of her Audrey. Call me if you need anything at all." I say and hug my sister tight enough for both women.

George and Mabel agreed to take care of the apartment while Tracey was gone. That is a big relief too. She will at least have a clean home to come back to if she decides to. This next journey for her is going to be a tough one. Her parents and Audrey will make sure she gets through it. I am the last person she needs to be around or worry about.

****

"Aiden, that is terrible. Poor girl. I should have gone around checking on her too." Mom says as I replay the afternoon's events for her in the kitchen of the 6AB. She hands me a beer and I can't help but take a long drink because today really has been an emotional roller coaster. "Have you told Karlie about this? I bet she would like to know there really isn't a baby on the way."

"I haven't really had much time to think about Karlie. I should call her but she will be home in a few days. I don't want to run after her and bring her home like I did last time. I need to come up with a better plan this time. This will be the LAST time. Any ideas?" I say and sit down on the barstool next to hers. I feel as if I haven't slept in weeks and can barely keep myself upright.

"Son, you look like you could pass out right here. Maybe you should go home and get some rest before you plan this big surprise. You haven't been sleeping well since Karlie left have you?" she asks with that motherly stern look on her face. How does she always know things like that? Must be a mother thing.

"You know Mom, you're right. I will talk to you all tomorrow. I am beat." I give Mom a big hug and kiss on the cheek before walking to my pickup and driving home to the AK. It feels so much easier to drive into the ranch now that I know there isn't anything keeping Karlie and I apart any longer. But first I need some sleep.

18

"Hi Mom. Karlie's plane gets in at 10:15 and I'll be here waiting for her with the limo. Yes, Ella Mae gave me Karlie's extra car key and Austin is on his way back with it right now. Yes, I am where she will see me once she exits the airport. She can't miss me Mom. Yes, then we will go have a picnic at the park with the pond and I will explain it all to her then. My sign will get her attention believe me. Thanks Mom. Bye." I hang up my phone and check my watch for the time. It's almost 10:15; the plane should be landing any minute now. Then if I know Karlie, she won't have any baggage, just a carry on so she won't have to go to baggage claim. I lean against the side of the limo holding on tight to my sign and my control as the butterflies and emotions try to overtake me. I am here awaiting the love of my life and I just pray she is as excited to see me as I will be to see her.

****

I'm not sure if I m excited to be home or not. Colvin just doesn't feel the same as it did before I lost Aiden. But I guess no time like the present to find out because as I walk off the plane and down the ramp I am hit with the reality that the last time I exited this plane, it was to come back to help with my Dad. I never dreamed he would pass away or that I would reconnect with Aiden. Now, I go home to Mom and Mom only.

Luckily, I don't have any baggage, just my carry on. I can head straight out of this madhouse airport and get my car. Then I will have a hundred miles to compose myself before I enter Colvin, land of Aiden Blake.

I step outside the automatic doors and am taken aback by what I see. The most handsome man ever and a sign that reads:

LOVE YOU ALWAYS!!

What is Aiden doing here? And with that sign? How did he know when my plane got in today? Mom…. That must be why she was so chipper when I talked to her earlier when we landed. She was part of this plan. I am not sure how I feel about this, she knows how upset I am about the baby and now she helps him come here to meet me.

"What are you doing here Aiden?" seeing him after being apart the last few weeks has really affected me more than I thought it ever would. My heart is beating so fast and I can barely breathe. My hands are shaking but I clasp them harder around my carry on and purse.

"I came to get you and take you home. I have missed you so much! Let's go." He says also sounding breathless and nervous. He ushers me towards the open limo door and I step into the car to sit on the seat. I have been in hundreds of limos over the years but this one seems to send me in a tailspin. I look around to see that it has flowers all over and sparkling water in glass bottles alongside of chocolate covered strawberries. My favorite. He still remembers. Of course he does. It's Aiden.

"But I have my own car that I need to get and head home." I say hesitantly as he climbs in beside me taking up most of the seat. I can feel his shoulder rub against my arm making goose bumps raise on my arms.

"Nope, Austin is probably about home in it as we speak." He pours a glass and hands it to me. He is enjoying this way too much.

"You thought of everything." I say and take a big drink of my water. I didn't realize I had such a dry mouth. Another affect Aiden has on me.

"Yep. Austin and Ella Mae were a lot of help in getting this plan executed. Now sit back and relax. We are going to a special spot for lunch." He sits back himself and takes a drink the smile never fading from his face.

I can't help but look at the love of my life and wonder if this is real. Wonder what he is doing here and how he thinks this is okay when he has a baby on the way with his ex.

****

Arriving at our lunch destination at the park with a pond, I grab the blanket and picnic basket out of the front seat. I spread the blanket out and sit. Patting the spot across from me, I look up at Karlie and see so much emotion on her face. She isn't sure what to do. She looks like she is ready to run. "Please sit down; I have a lot I need to say before you run in the other direction."

She sits down cautiously and quickly folds her hands in her lap. If I didn't know better I would think she were scared. Time to spit it out.

"A lot happened since you left for Miami. Audrey and I found Tracey one afternoon in her bedroom and she had almost over dosed. She has been doing Heroine since our engagement news spread around town. And she was only faking the pregnancy in hopes to get me back. Audrey helped her get to Dallas and her parents put her into rehab. That is why I am here today Karlie, I need you to know that I still love you more than anything and want to marry you as planned in a couple weeks. If you will have me." I say and reach for her hand unsure if she would allow me to touch her or not. She does. The look on her face tells it all. She is beyond overwhelmed with the information.

As we sample all of the good food that Mom and Ella Mae have sent with me, I answer all the questions she has. The more time that goes by, I start to realize that our future might actually be attainable.

****

Aiden explained the entire Tracey situation during lunch and as we drive back to Colvin, I can't help but sit here still a little stunned. He isn't angry with her but I'm not sure I can be that forgiving. Yes, I know she was going through her own little Hell but that doesn't mean I have to be okay with her ruining the past several weeks of my life. Right?

I look over at Aiden and all of those prior thoughts seem so insignificant. I am so happy to find out that Aiden still loves me and that our future is still the same as it was before all of this drama. I didn't realize just how much I missed him until he leaned over and kissed me senseless before we took off towards home in the limo.

We made love in the limo and it felt like it had been years not weeks since our last touch. I don't want to spend another Moment not being able to touch Aiden. I agreed to move back into the AK and move forward with the wedding plans. I would imagine between his family and my Mom my stuff is moved and ready for us before we even get home. When I called Mom a few minutes ago, she was ecstatic. I thought our families are just as happy that we are back on track. That feels so good to say. Back on track.

****

I lay here watching Karlie as she talks on the phone with her Mom and my heart feels so full of love for this woman. I almost lost the ability to see her smile and hear that laugh of hers. She is the most beautiful and passionate woman I have ever met and thankfully I will soon be able to call her my wife. In a few weeks she will walk down that aisle towards me and we will exchange I do's. That day can't come soon enough.

She hangs up her phone, smiles and leans into me to press her lips against mine and says, "How far are we from home?"

I reach up with both arms and pull her close knowing her real meaning to that question. I could stay in this backseat all day if that's what it took to be able to make love to Karlie over and over again.

19

A few weeks later.....

Karlie is working in her downtown Colvin studio when the door opens and in comes her soldier brother and a tall blonde that looks all too familiar.

"Jonathan what are you doing here?" I say quickly but forget to mask my feelings for the next part, "And with Tracey Wheeler?"

"We were just going to get a cup of coffee after running into each other at the post office." He says with eyes pleading for me to be nice. "I just wanted to stop by and ask when I have to try on this monkey suit I am told I have to wear. The things I do for you girl."

"Thank you. You can go try it on at the tux shop any time before Saturday. By the way, how long are you home?" Karlie asks trying to ignore the fact that Aiden's ex is with her brother.

"Only a couple of days. There's some stuff in Charlotte I have to take care of before I can decide my next move." He says and kisses my cheek.

"Thank you for coming home to walk me down the aisle. It means the world to me and to Aiden." She says hugging her brother once more really feeling the tension in the room.

"I would do anything for you sis, you know that. And I really like Aiden." He smiles and looks at Tracey unaware of the connection she has with his soon to be brother-in-law. "Well, we better get our coffee. See you at Mom's tonight for dinner. Love you sis."

"Bye, love you. See you then." I say as I try to wrap my head around the fact that my brother is having a date with Tracey, of all people. Just coffee. Not a date. Right?

****

"It fits perfectly." I say tears forming in my eyes as I look at myself in the full length mirror inside the bridal salon. I am here for my final dress fitting before the wedding this weekend. I can't believe I am finally marrying Aiden. This dress is exquisite and I couldn't be happier.

Our colors are silver and creamy white so this dress is in that creamy white shade with silver jewels accentuating the curves of it. This is the most beautiful dress I have ever seen and love it so much. I helped to design it and can't believe how great it turned out. Aiden is going to love it.

"How are you wearing your hair?" Audrey asks from behind me. "Aiden is going to flip out when he sees you walking down the aisle in this Karlie. It is absolutely stunning."

"Thank you Audrey for all of your help with the wedding. I really am glad you agreed to be my maid of honor. Savannah will be here tomorrow to be the other bride's maid." I say hugging her before returning to the dressing room to change.

"Um, I need to ask you something. Is Tracey dating anyone? I know she is still living in Dallas and going to rehab and all but, she came in the studio with Jonathan earlier today." I say as I walk out carrying the dress and handing it to the seamstress.

"No, but she did tell me she ran into him and had coffee. Are you ok with that?" she asks knowing enough to realize I might not be with everything that happened a few weeks ago.

"I really don't know Audrey. She almost cost me and Aiden our future. I have a hard time with anything Tracey. Now with my brother?" I say making a strange face that makes Audrey laugh.

"But he is marrying you in two days. Tracey doesn't matter anymore to Aiden. He got his girl, remember?" she says making me feel so much better. At the Moment anyway. "Let's go. We have flowers to finalize with Austin at the nursery."

****

Later that night as Aiden and I pull up to my Mom's house for dinner we see that Tracey's car is also there and I see Aiden get the crease in his forehead when he is unsure about something.

"What is she doing here?"

"She had coffee today with Jonathan and I guess it must have gone well." I say trying to sound upbeat about the idea. "Let's get inside before Mom comes out yelling for us."

"This ought to be interesting." Aiden says under his breath and opens the front door.

"Hi guys! So glad to see you could make it! Jonathan is in the kitchen finishing his famous guacamole dip. Go on in!"

"Mom it smells wonderful! I had a dress fitting during lunch so I didn't have time to eat." I say as I use a chip to scoop some of the dip into my mouth while covertly looking around for Tracey.

"Did it go ok? No issues?" Mom asks while taking the enchiladas out of the oven. She has always made the best enchiladas. "Aiden, I think a fuse is out in my car, could you check on that for me?"

As he walks towards the door leading to the garage he smiles an uneasy smile. I know what he is thinking. Where is she? That's the same thing I am thinking.

"It all fit great. The extra mile I run every morning has helped to fight off the bulge."

"It's not just the running that's working off those calories Karlie!" Aiden says with a smile and a wink before slipping into the garage.

"You two that's enough! Get a room would you? The rest of us don't need a visual!" Jonathan says and throws the dish towel at me.

"So, I take it your date went well?"

"Yes, it did why do you say it like that?"

"I saw her car out front." I say quickly. "Where is she?"

"Jonathan's car didn't get finished at the repair shop yet and since he's meeting Tracey for coffee later, she offered him her car." Mom says smiling completely unaware of my discomfort.

"Thanks Mom but I can talk for myself. What do you have against her anyway Karlie? I saw the way you acted around her and treated her in the studio today." He asks knowing he is missing something big.

"You really don't know? How can you not know? Oh yeah, you were in Iraq still.

"She and Aiden were together for three years before I came back. She thought they were going to get married and live happily ever after. Then, a few weeks ago she came to Aiden and told her she was pregnant. That's when I went to Miami. But come to find out she was faking and also struggling with a drug addiction." I say while fighting back all of those emotions from that time. It still hurts to remember.

"Whoa. I didn't know that. I guess I understand now why you were so cold to her. We are just friends anyway." he says putting his hands up for a truce.

"I don't hate her. It's just awkward being around her." I say with too much emotion that causes Mom to come hug me from behind. "He cared about her too and if I hadn't have come back before Dad died; I would have lost Aiden forever. And a few weeks ago, please don't make me remember."

"Do you have a problem with me dating her? Well, if you call it dating. I am going back to Charlotte in a few days anyway." He says and pulls me into a hug before I could get mad or answer him but I pull away to answer.

"I don't know Jonathan. It's just weird. Have you talked to her about it? I guess not if you didn't know." I say with a sassy tone. "This is just weird, can we eat now?"

While we are carrying everything into the dining room for dinner, Aiden emerges from the garage and walks to the sink to wash his hands. Suddenly I realize that I am so thankful he wasn't in the room for that conversation. We don't really talk about his past with Tracey. He knows it's too tough for me to talk about. Maybe her dating someone else would be a good thing. But my brother? My brother....

I walk to Aiden and hug him from behind and fill him in on the Tracey story before we join the others in the dining room.

"Baby, I'm sorry this is all getting drug back up again." He says as he turns around and pulls me into his arms.

"I know it's just a sore spot for me when I see her. To think she could have been the one marrying you this weekend." I say pouting, but realizing how close I did come to losing Aiden. Twice.

"You are my missing piece, remember?" Aiden says as he kisses my forehead. "Can we eat now?"

I just smile and shake my head as we walk to the dining room hand in hand.

20

Friday night I am picked up in a limo by Audrey and a few other ladies. It's time for my bachelorette party while Aiden is having his bachelor party at the 6AB Ranch with the guys.

He helped me pick out my dress for tonight and then of course Audrey pulled out something much shorter and much more revealing once we left. As I get the dress on, the limo heads off the ranch and I soon get a text from Aiden telling me he knows she had something else for me to wear and it didn't really matter what it was as long as he was the one that got to take it off of me at the end of the night.

I smile and accept the drink from Audrey and toast to an exciting night with the girls for the last time as a single woman. I just can't wait until tomorrow evening when I become Aiden's wife.

"Are you ready for the first phase of the night?" asks Audrey with a suspicious grin from ear to ear. "This is going to be a night you will never forget Karlie!"

"Audrey, you do remember that Ella Mae and I are with you girls, right?" Amelia says questioning the content of the plans Audrey has made.

"Yes Mom, I know you ladies are with us too. Are you worried about what I have planned will be too young for your blood?"

"No young lady I am not saying we are too old for bachelorette parties; just making sure it's going to be G rated. You can be quite ornery!" Amelia says trying not to crack too big of a smile towards Audrey.

"Ok Audrey, what do you have planned? Let's get this night over with so I can get married tomorrow!"

Audrey looks out the limo window and says, "Looks like we are here. Leave your purses ladies, no money or ID's needed tonight."

Mom, Amelia, Savannah and I look around at each other with an uneasiness that matched from face to face while Audrey sits there looking as if she were a cat who just caught a big fat bird.

"Seriously Audrey? A bar? Isn't this tacky?" I say pleading with her as we get out and see that she has taken us to the only bar in town. "This is all you could come up with?"

"Just keep an open mind would ya? I won't let you down, I promise." And with that she heads to the door and we all follow dreading what lies ahead of us.

"Ladies, welcome to Vegas! Please know that what happens in Vegas, stays in Vegas!" Audrey flings the door open and ushers the rest of us in.

As we walk into the bar it is spectacularly turned into a casino straight from the Strip. It has slot machines, poker tables, roulette wheels, Elvis, showgirls, mimes, sparkling decorations hanging everywhere, and even cocktail waitresses that greet us with glasses full of bubbly champagne and try to get a grip on exactly what Audrey has done here. It's amazing and way over the top.

"Audrey how in the world did you pull all of this off without anyone knowing? This is amazing!" I say not able to keep the smile off of my face and fling my arms around my soon to be sister in law.

"I just thought it was time the women had a night out on the strip. So I brought the Strip to Colvin! It's 8:30 now and at 11:30 sharp your next surprise will be here. So please, live it up in Vegas!"

I decide at that Moment that Audrey did an amazing thing and it was time for us to enjoy every Moment of it. These types of things don't happen every day and not many brides to be are presented with such an amazing bachelorette party. Time to let go of the uneasiness and live it up Vegas style!

"So, who wants to play poker? The men aren't the only ones who can play poker tonight!" I say smiling and gesturing for the others to join me at the table.

****

After too many glasses of champagne, several pulls on the slots, and several hands of poker which my mother surprisingly won every one of, it is nearing 11:30 and I turn to Audrey to see what she has planned next. Just as I start to say something to her, the music changes and out come men dressed as policemen, firefighters, executives, cowboys, etc. What has she done? I do not want to see naked men!

"Audrey, please tell me these aren't male strippers! You know this is not something I want to do. Audrey, please no."

"Karlie, you really don't want them? I thought it would be funny. I didn't mean to upset you. Do you want me to tell them to leave?" she asks and we both turn to see my mother sitting on the policeman's lap with a smile the size of Texas on her face. "I think your Mom would disagree!"

"Oh my. Yes, I'm afraid you are right. You know what? Call all your girlfriends and have them meet you here. Someone might as well enjoy themselves. I would rather go home and see Aiden anyways. Is that ok with you Audrey?"

"You and Aiden have something that everyone is looking for. Go home and be with him. Just remember, you can't stay with him tonight. He can't see you before the ceremony. I will make sure your Mom gets home okay."

"I love you Audrey. Bye!" I run off towards the waiting limo. "Take me home please."

When I arrive home I see that the lights are all still on up on the hill at the 6AB so the bachelor party must still be going on. Oh well, I would rather be home than with those half naked strangers anyways. I will just wait for him to get home. Surely he won't be long.

I decide to grab a glass of wine and head out back on the deck and can't help but stare at the creek. I wish my father were here to enjoy the wedding festivities. Most of all I wish he were here to walk me down the aisle. Mom would love to have him here too I am sure to share in the parents of the bride role. It seems like just yesterday that I talked to Dad about Aiden. He must have known all along that this day would be coming. Even when we were so blind. He always knew. Always hoped.

I start to relax and let the memories flood me and start to feel comforted knowing Dad will always be here at the AK even if only there on the creek bank.

****

I know my little sister had a much sexier dress for Karlie to wear out tonight, but Audrey doesn't need to know that I do. As long as I get to take it off Karlie, whatever she wears is fine. Tomorrow she becomes my wife and I can't wait.

As I watch the limo drive away carrying the most important women in my life I realize how blessed and excited I am to be exactly who I am. I wouldn't change a thing that has led Karlie and me up to this point. Yes, it was a bit of a mess but we are getting married tomorrow. Now if I can just get through tonight and to the ceremony so that I can see her. We haven't spent any nights apart since I flew to LA to tell her I loved her and proposed to her.

I climb into my pickup and head towards the 6AB up on the hill. The lights in the barn are bright and I can hear lots of male laughter and smell cigar smoke before I enter. As I do, I see Dad, Austin, Jonathan, and even Aaron has made it home from his business trip to New York in time. Everyone is here and ready to get some poker on.

"Let's get the cigars burning and the cards shuffling! I have a bride to get to tomorrow!" I say smiling and slapping my hand on the poker table before sitting down. "Thank you all for coming. It means the world to me."

"Aiden, we wouldn't want to be anywhere else but here with you. We are very happy and relieved to know you and Karlie are finally on the same page. We were beginning to think your books were from different genres for awhile!" Austin says as he sits down takes a big swig of his beer. The rest of the men follow suit and the cards are dealt.

****

"You do know that once you say "I do" tomorrow things are going to change right? No more freedom. Karlie will have you just where she wants you." Says Jonathan with a wicked grin on his face as he raises the bet.

"Jonathan, your sister can have me anywhere or anyway she wants me!" I say laughing so hard I spill my beer on my lap. "And I don't want freedom; I have wanted your sister since I was five. It's about time I get what I want right?"

"Sure man. You keep telling yourself that! I am never getting tied down by one woman no matter what!" Aaron says while he and Jonathan agree and toast their mugs of beer together.

"You have been seeing a lot of Tracey, what are you spouting off about?" I say knowing I couldn't keep the grin off my face. "Looks like you are close to being tied down."

"I am enjoying her company yes, nothing more. I leave for Iraq again in a couple days so this is definitely not the time for a relationship. And who wants one woman?" Jonathan says while folding his hand.

"I have been married to the same woman for over 35 years Jonathan. I have to say it's better than what you are picturing or have heard. Your ma and pa were married for almost that too so where did this sour notion of relationships come from?" my Dad says breaking his silence and snuffing out his cigar.

"I have just seen so many couples not survive the separation that being away at war brings. So many of the guys I see every day and every night have received divorce decrees in their care packages. They are crushed and seem to change from that Moment. It's just too much. Maybe after my time is up, but for now, no thanks."

"Ok, so let's do one more round and then I would like to go home and see my bride to be. At least I hope Audrey has let her go by now. She brought the skimpiest dress for Karlie to change into after they left. I would hate to miss seeing that thing on her." I say smiling and so excited to go home to Karlie. "Aaron, would you mind taking me home?"

"Sure little brother. It's about time you got home to Karlie. You don't want to miss your last rendezvous as a single man and single woman." He says while slapping me on the back and heading for the door.

"Thanks guys for coming, see you all at Ella Mae's house tomorrow!"

"Could you get a smaller car Aaron? How does this one handle the dirt roads anyway?" I ask as I slip inside and shut the door just as he has done the same and started the engine.

"She really purrs doesn't she? She does just fine on the dirt road and no more often than I am on them, who cares?" Aaron says with a smile as we head towards my part of the ranch.

"You ever going to move home full time? You have to be sick of the big city Aaron. Dad could really use your help on the ranch you know since Austin has taken on so much more responsibility at the nursery and with me having my own ranch too."

"Aiden, you know I love being in the big city and would hate being here full time. The country life isn't for me. Never has been. If Dad needs help, hire new guys. Surely others would love to work here. I can help screen applicants before I go back to Denver."

"Night brother. See you tomorrow. Thanks for the ride. And thanks again for all the amazing work you did on KAB." I say shaking his hand and jumping out to run inside very anxious to see Karlie. As I do, I see that she is home too. I walk inside and see her standing on the back deck looking out at the creek.

When I get closer I see her turn around and I am stricken with how beautiful this woman is. She is standing there skin aglow and chestnut hair falling over her shoulders wearing a tight and short, very short, black dress with sparkles all over it. Her high strappy heels accentuate her great long legs and I notice she is wearing no jewelry except my ring on her left hand. She is the most beautiful woman I have ever seen and feel so dizzy knowing I get to go to sleep beside her every night and wake up to her every morning for the rest of my life.

I walk to her and wrap my left arm around her waist pulling her close as I put my right hand behind her head and touch my lips to hers. I convey in this kiss just how much I feel for this woman and for our future together.

"How was your night?" I ask finally breaking off the hottest kiss I have ever felt. "I didn't think you would be home this early."

"I wanted to see you before I went to Mom's. You can't see me after tonight until I walk down the aisle." She says wrapping her arms around my waist and laying her head against my chest.

"I have to spend the night alone?" I ask pleading with her to change her mind with a kiss and pulling her against my hard body so that she can feel how she is affecting me.

"I have a bit of time before it gets too late. But then I do have to go." She says as she steps back and takes off her heels one foot at a time smiling sexily.

I walk up to her and turn her around and start to unzip her dress and kiss her shoulders and bare back. She whimpers and I drop the dress to see her gorgeous body clad in only a matching lacy bra and panties. I can't take much of this so I pick her up and head upstairs to make the most of our last night before we become husband and wife.

21

Opening my eyes I can see the sun's rays fighting their way into the room. Looking around the room, the room I was brought to as a newborn, I see my life and self in a new way. I was very fortunate to have two amazing parents and brother to show me all that I am. I am so sad that Dad won't be here to walk me down the aisle. I always dreamed that he would be. I guess every girl dreams of that. I know today is going to be hard on all of us knowing he isn't here. My heart aches thinking about Mom being alone through this and since I moved to the AK but at least Jonathan is here for now. Maybe he will be back home soon. I am very thankful he is here today to do Dads job. My Dad can't be here then Jonathan is the next best.

Thinking of my wedding this afternoon makes the butterflies start to flutter and I can't help but smile. I didn't think I would ever get to this day and say "I do" to Aiden. I will finally be his wife. And to that a big smile covers my face.

Knock. Knock. Knock

"Come in." I say as I hear the familiar three knocks that Jonathan has done for as long as I can remember.

"How's the bride doing this morning? Nervous?"

"Great and no, actually."

"We weren't sure you were going to stay here last night when you weren't here when we both got home." He says with a wicked smile. "I can't imagine where you were."

"No where important." I say smiling so big my face hurt.

"Ya right. After Aiden left his own bachelor party early I didn't expect to see u at all! Mom was a bit nervous with the superstition and all." Jonathan says while pulling something out of his pocket. "I want you to have this pin today for your something borrowed, old and blue. Dad gave this guardian Angel pin to me before I left for boot camp and I thought you would like it for today. You can't keep it since I'm going back to Iraq and all but I will loan it to you for today."

"Jonathan I love it!!! I will pin it on my bouquet and will carry you and Dad with me with pride! Thank you so much!!" I say and jump up to give him a big hug.

"I love you Karlie Mae. I'm so happy for you and Aiden. I'm also very honored to be the one taking Dad's place walking you down the aisle to Aiden." Jonathan says and kisses my forehead and walks out my door shutting it behind him.

I stand here looking at this angel pin and I envision Dad giving it to Jonathan. I remember the day he left like it was yesterday. Dad was so proud of him while Mom and I just cried.

I wonder what Dad would say to me today if he were here. I know he would be happy I am marrying Aiden. I'm just sorry it took us this long.

****

"Ok, so I just talked to the caterers and the band. They are all set. Reverend Lowell will be here about 3:30 and the tables and chairs are being set up now. Austin said the flowers are ready to deliver too from Stampley's Nursery so I believe that is the last of it."

"Breathe, Mom. It will all be fine. But thank you so much for all you have done. Now it's time for you to sit down and enjoy the day." I give her a big hug and try to calm her frazzled nerves. "I thought it was the bride who was supposed to be stressed out today?"

"Karlie Mae I just want everything to be perfect for your big day. Without your father here it's important to me to make it as special as he and I had always talked about."

"It will be perfect Mom, don't worry anymore. Let the professionals do what we have paid them to do. Let's get you some lunch!" I say heading to the kitchen to make us all some food. "Where's Jonathan by the way?"

"I'm not sure; he said he had some things to take care of before the wedding. He said he would be back in plenty of time to walk you down the aisle."

"Hmmmmm. Turkey or ham, Mom?" I ask knowing I have too much else to worry about than what my brother is up to.

****

Ding dong. Ding dong.

Who would he here this early? I told Mom I would come up there to get ready for the wedding. It's barely noon....

Opening the front door I see its Jonathan. "Hey man, what's up? Is something wrong with Karlie or Ella Mae?" I say a little worried.

"Everyone is fine. I just wanted to stop by today before all the hoopla starts." He says with a smile. "I was hoping I could go down by the creek a bit if you don't mind."

"Of course, you don't have to ask. Your sister lives here and after tonight it's going to be her land too. Even though you are always welcome. I know that's where you both feel Gene the most, so you go anytime you like." I say knowing today is hard for everyone without Gene.

"Thanks. I just feel such pressure to stand in for him where Mom and Karlie are concerned and today is definitely no exception. I know Dad would be so happy and proud that you two are getting married, but it's still a lot of pressure."

Knowing he needs time alone, I head back to my room to finish gathering up my stuff. I should be nervous but I actually am very at ease. That is until I get to Moms. I chuckle to myself and concentrate on the task at hand.

****

"Aiden are you on your way yet? You are going to be late to your own wedding and Ella Mae will ring your neck!"

With a big smile I answer, "Yes Mom, I just pulled up out front."

"Oh good!!" She exclaims and hangs up already running out of the front door towards me.

"It's 2 o'clock young man! Are you trying to give me a coronary? Your father and brothers and Audrey are already ready to go and we aren't the ones getting married today!" She says giving me a stern look and opening the pickup door for me.

"Calm down, all I have to do is get my tux on and go to town. What are you so stressed out for? Isn't it the bride who is supposed to be all stressed out today?" I say trying to hurry inside with my stuff to get changed. Even though I know we have two hours before the ceremony starts.

"Aiden, just get ready please. Your father and I want to leave soon." And with that she storms away making me chuckle to myself again.

I hope Karlie isn't this stressed out. She hasn't been a Bridezilla yet, I hope she isn't now. I decide to text her to see and let her know I love her.

How are you? Mom is freaking out on me. All good here. I love you.

I start to put on my tux and hear my phone chime for a text. That must be Karlie.

I am great. Mom is freaking out too. Love you so much more.

I doubt that but it's good to hear she is doing fine. Why are our mothers so on edge? Couldn't be that they have waited eight and a half years for this day could it? That makes me smile.

Finishing up my bow tie, I hear Dad say from behind me, "You look dashing, son. Gene would be very proud and happy that you are marrying his daughter. I believe he is smiling down from heaven today. Love you."

"Thanks Dad. I think he would be too. Love you." I say giving him a hug. I don't know what I would do if it were my Dad not here to enjoy today with me. Poor Ella Mae it has to be super tough on her not having her husband to share in the joy of watching their daughter get married today.

****

I'm out front. You have them with you in backyard?

I send a quick text to Austin as I pull up in Karlie's driveway. We are having the wedding in their backyard and Austin has a special bouquet for Ella Mae that I want to deliver before the wedding starts.

Yep. You deliver or me?

I get a fast response. He must have been waiting for my call.

Is Ella Mae out there with you?

Nope. I will go tell her you want her back

here for a sec.

I walk through the side gate of the yard and I am just blown away at what I see. Their backyard was gorgeous before but this is unbelievable. It's like a whole different place. Karlie is going to love this.

"Aiden? Your brother said you needed me for a second? Do you not like something?" I hear Ella Mae say coming up behind me.

I turn, smile and hug her while saying, "It's beautiful Ella Mae! I just wanted to give you a little something before the wedding started. I had this bouquet made for you because I know that Gene always brought you yellow tulips on special days because they're your favorite. And since he isn't here to do that today, I wanted to make sure you still got them. There is a small picture of him hanging from the ribbon just like Karlie's so you will have him with you today."

"Oh Aiden!! I am so happy you are marrying our daughter today and finally joining our family. Gene loved you as if you were his other son. This is the most thoughtful thing, thank you so much."

"Ok well now you better go take care of my bride. I can't wait until I can call her my wife and am proud to become an official part of your family." I say proudly while giving her one last hug and letting her walk back towards the house where I know my bride is getting ready. I don't think I have ever been so happy.

****

"Reverend Lowell, how are you?" I ask seeing him stepping into the hallway outside the room where I am getting ready.

"It is almost 3:45 so I wanted to check on you one last time before I took my place outside. You look beautiful Karlie Mae!" Reverend Lowell says looking genuinely pleased. "The yard looks amazing too."

"Thank you so much for being here today and agreeing to marry Aiden and me. We couldn't have asked anyone else. You have known us our whole lives therefore we found you to be the best fit for today."

"Well if you are all set in here then I will find Aiden and the guys. See you out there."

After the reverend walks away I can't help but replay events in my life that have led me to this day. All of the mistakes I have made have paved the way for my being able to marry Aiden today. If I hadn't have left for LA like I did I wouldn't be the person I am today either. Aiden and I were meant to be together but not until now. That was always hard to understand but call it wedding bliss or whatever, I clearly see it now. In less than twenty minutes I am going to finally marry the man I have loved the majority of my life. I don't think I have ever been so happy.

22

Mom and I are standing inside the patio doors awaiting our queue to walk towards Jonathan and of course Aiden. The backyard has been transformed into a fairy tale with white lights and cream colored flowers of all kinds. There is sparkle and magic everywhere I look. The chairs are covered in silver fabric and tied with cream colored bows on the backs. Cream fabric and clear lights are draped over head to create a ceiling. Aiden is standing there hands behind his back and a content smile in a black tux. He looks so sexy up there. It takes all I have not to run to him. I have missed not being able to see him since last night.

No one can see us yet but we can see them. All of our friends and family have shown up today to witness our union. I can't think of a person that isn't here that should be. That is except Dad. I touch the pin on my bouquet right beside the picture that Aiden put there for me of Dad. "Well Dad this is it."

Mom opens the doors and I see everyone turn my way. The only person I see is Aiden standing at the end of the aisle with Reverend Lowell. I feel the emotion trying to bubble to the surface as I walk towards Jonathan. He takes my hand and Mom goes to her seat in the front leaving us alone to venture on.

"I love you sis." Jonathan says with a smile and squeezes my arm. "You ready?"

All I can so is nod for the fear of tears escaping if I try to speak. With that confirmation we begin the slow walk to my future. To Aiden.

****

The patio doors open and I get the first glimpse of the most beautiful bride I have ever seen. Standing there in cream fabric that flows from her shoulders to the ground, she looks stunning. Her hair is swept up on one side and I see her smile from even this far away. She honestly took my breath away as she began her slow journey down the aisle towards me. Her skin is glowing and so is her face. I will never forget this vision as long as I live.

"Jonathan. Thank you." I say as they reach me and I take Karlie's arm from him. I want so bad to lean down and kiss her beautiful mouth but I know there is a time for that after we are pronounced man and wife. That seems like a million years away.

Squeezing her arm once to hopefully convey my feelings to her, we turn to face the reverend.

"Aiden and Karlie we are here today to witness your joining as man and wife. It has been a long journey to get to this alter today but the real and meaningful journey is about to begin. The love that the two of you share is priceless and very rare. Most men and women only dream of finding their soul mate. Not many find that soul mate as a child. The two of you were very blessed to have had that occur. While you both went about your own lives up until now, you were never far from each other's thoughts and hearts. This union was meant to be and therefore will be."

Aiden and I go through the ceremony fighting back tears and emotions as we pledge to spend the rest of our lives together.

"Karlie with this ring I promise to love you and cherish you every day for the rest of my life." And I slide her wedding band on her left ring finger. That band matches perfectly to the diamond ring I gave her in LA. Like they were meant to be just like she and I are.

"Aiden with this ring I promise to love you and cherish you every day for the rest of my life." And she slides my wedding band onto my left ring finger. As she does that I can't seem to keep the emotion at bay any longer and a few tears slip out.

"Aiden, Karlie, I have the great honor of being able to pronounce you husband and wife. Aiden you may kiss your beautiful bride." the reverend says and all I can think is thank goodness!

I wrap my arms around Karlie and she wraps hers around my neck meeting me in the middle with as much emotion as I have. As soon as our lips touch I could swear there are fireworks going off. This is the woman I get to call my wife for the rest of my life. How did I ever get so lucky?

****

As I wrap my arms around Aiden's neck and meet his lips with mine I am overcome with emotion because I just married the love of my life and get to call him my husband until the end of time. How did I ever get so lucky?

"We did it!" I whisper to him after the most powerful kiss we have ever had.

"Yes we did baby! You look beyond amazing and I love you so much!" He says pulling me tight against him again.

"You are the best thing that has ever happened to me. You do know that don't you?"

"I am pleased to introduce to you for the first time, Mr. And Mrs. Aiden Blake!" We hear the reverend announce and pull apart to walk back down the aisle. We can see and hear the love and joy from everyone in attendance. Everyone was clearly as moved with emotion as we were.

Aiden grabs my hand and we make our way to the back of the chairs and towards the patio doors. Mom and the rest of the crew will get the backyard transformed now into the reception area while Aiden and I meet with the reverend to sign the license and have a few minutes alone.

"The wedding was just beautiful you two. I am very proud to have been the one to officiate. Now, if you two can just sign here and here I will get you off to spend a few minutes alone as husband and wife and take your photos. I will get Jonathan to sign as your witness then it will all be legal. Congratulations." The reverend says handing Aiden the pen then me.

Aiden takes my hand and we head to what used to be my bedroom while growing up. He barely gets the door closed before I wrap my arms around his waist and lay my head against his chest. I can hear and feel his heart beating strongly and I know it beats with love for me.

He wraps his arms around me and sighs. "I can't believe we finally did it. We're married Karlie!"

I lift my head up and look straight into his eyes and say, "Aiden I love you so much and am so blessed to be able to call you my husband. Finally!"

He dips his head and catches my lips again for a searing kiss that promises to never fade. The kiss turns into several and things start to heat up as we hear three knocks on the door. Jonathan.

Knock. Knock. Knock

"Ok you two, enough alone time. Gerry is ready for us." Jonathan says and Aiden reluctantly opens the door.

Time to let the big city photographer have his way with us. I am so thankful Gerry agreed to come to Colvin and take our wedding photos. I couldn't think of anyone better for the job. I think he is actually liking small town Oklahoma. He seems a lot more laid back that I think I have ever seen him before. This town has a way of growing on you. I can attest to that.

"I am so grateful you agreed to come take the pictures, Gerry." I say and hug my mentor and friend.

"Well, I wouldn't trust anyone else to do it for my girl! Now, stop stalling and get over there with that handsome husband of yours!" he says and winks. "People are out there starving! I am one of them!"

****

"Please help me in welcoming for the first time, Aiden and Karlie Blake!" I hear the band leader say over the microphone. I take Karlie's hand and see she has a gorgeous smile on her face that radiates how happy she is today. It makes my heart swell because I am just as happy if not more.

It has been a magical night and I love looking out and seeing all of our family and friends enjoying themselves. After having the first dance with my wife, I sit down next to her awaiting the speeches. This should be interesting coming from Jonathan.

"I think I knew the day that Dad brought Karlie Mae out to the 6AB with us that even at 5 years old she and Aiden were destined to be together. That day seems like yesterday but now my little sister is all grown up and I had the greatest pleasure of walking her down the aisle today. While we all would have loved to have had Dad here to do it himself, I was very blessed to be asked in his place. May the two of you be just as blessed if not much more for the rest of your years to come. Oh, and I would like nieces and nephews soon!" Jonathan says in a speech that brought tears to everyone's eyes. I stand and hug him with all the emotion I have.

"Thank you." That is all I am able to get out before I break down in tears. Happy tears of course.

Aiden seeing this is too hard for me stands and says, "That day was the best day of my life until today when I saw you bringing the most beautiful woman I have ever seen towards me. Thank you for entrusting me with your sister and your daughter Ella Mae. And most definitely you Gene in heaven." He says and raises his glass towards heaven. All I can do is raise my glass too and know Dad is up there raising his glass with us.

"I will see what I can do about those nieces and nephews Jonathan!" Aiden says and everyone laughs out loud changing the mood back to a celebration. That is one of the reasons I love this man so much. He always knows what to say or do at just the right moment.

Aiden sits down again and pulls me in for another kiss. With that kiss I tried to pour all of my emotion and love into it so that he knew without a doubt how I feel.

****

At the end of the night and after many guests' congratulations, we are starting to make our way out of the reception when we are stopped by a voice from behind us, "That was a beautiful wedding you two. I am very happy for you. I pray you always feel as happy and in love as you do right now." Tracey says and turns to walk away. We both say thank you and look at each other not really sure if that just happened or not.

"She looks like she is doing better doesn't she?"

"She deserves the best for showing me how much I loved you." Aiden says back. "Mrs. Blake are you ready to sneak out of here? I have a surprise for you before we leave for Fiji."

"Fiji?? Are you serious?" she asks as her face lights up with a smile forgetting all about the surprise part.

"You gave up Fiji to come home with me from LA so I thought that was the most fitting place we could go on our honeymoon." I say while pulling my wife into my arms. How right does that feel being able to call her my wife?

"Why Mr. Blake you are full of surprises! Yes, let's go!" she says giggling as we run out the door before anyone can see us leaving.

****

I drive us to the ranch and to our special creek. As we drive up I see that Karlie has tears threatening to spill out of her eyes. I reach over and grasp her hand. I kiss the palm of her delicate hand and thank God for showing me who I was meant to spend the rest of my life with.

"Aiden you brought me to the creek where it all began… I feel closest to Dad here and you knew I was missing him didn't you?"

"Karlie there is a reason I own this part of the ranch. I bought it because it was the most special spot to me because of you. I brought you here tonight to ease your heart about missing Gene today. He was there and I think this is the best place for us to feel him. I just hope he approves of me marrying his baby. I had a plaque made and mounted here on the creek bank commemorating your Dad. Now when you are missing him, you can just come down to the creek and not only feel his presence, but see him also."

"Aiden I am so very thankful for you. I have wanted to be with you for most of my life and now I am able to go to sleep beside you every night and wake up and see your smile first thing every morning. I love you!"

Just as she said that a slight breeze blew through the trees and a fish jumped in the water letting us know that Gene approved and it was his way of showing us just what we were seeking and what Karlie desperately needed.

"Well there's our answer! Now let's get out of here and go on that honeymoon you chose so we can start making little Blake's. I can't wait to get you all to myself."

"Karlie Mae Doone how could I have ever been so lucky to have a woman like you? I can't wait to see you pregnant with my children. Can we work on that now or do we really have to go?"

"Hey, it's Blake now! Let's go before we miss our flight to Fiji!! I don't want to miss out on it a second time. We can work on the pregnant part once we get there!!"

"It will be so much better this time, you won't be working. You won't be wearing much clothing either. You might not see as many sites except the bedroom, but it will be worth it!"

"And I will be there with my husband, the love of my life, and best friend! No matter where we are will be worth it as long as I have you by my side. I love you!"

Epilogue

"Well, look at the happy couple. You two look tan and relaxed after your honeymoon." Austin says as he walks into his Mom's kitchen and finds Aiden and Karlie there fresh from their trip to Fiji. "You look like you were gone longer than a week."

"It felt like we were gone a day. It went by so fast!" pouts Karlie as she hands Austin a folder. "The wedding photos from Gerry juts arrived. The flowers were gorgeous Austin!"

"I agree. It was a beautiful wedding and reception you two. Congrats, again." Austin says opening the folder and eyeing the wonderful photos inside. "These are amazing. No wonder you are so good if he was the one who mentored you. Wow."

"They are wonderful aren't they?" Austin's Mom, Amelia, says with so much pride. "It was just so beautiful! This one is my favorite, the one of you two on the patio in front of all the flowers and sparkle behind you. It looks so magical."

"Thank you all so much for all the hard work and time you put into making our wedding so amazing. You will never know how much it means to the both of us." Aiden says pulling his new wife close to his side and kisses her temple. "That one is our favorite too Mom. We are going to have it blown up and framed for your wall and one for ours. Austin these are for you to use however you want at Stampley's. They show just what an amazing job you did."

"It was just another day on the job. You do know I do flowers for a living right?" Austin says smiling at his little brother. "I am actually thinking of talking to Jack about buying Stampley's. These will definitely help win him over."

"Austin, that would be great! How long have you been thinking about this?" Amelia asks with so much excitement for her son.

"I sat around the wedding before the guests arrived and it just kinda hit me. I love doing this and have been for so long that I needed to take the next step. I am planning on talking to Jack about it soon. Do you really think it is a good idea?" Austin asks of his family members present.

"Of course we do! You did such a wonderful job with our wedding flowers and I have seen those you have done other places. You have a gift and you should secure it because Jack won't be around forever." Karlie says squeezing Austin's arm from beside him.

"She's absolutely right Austin. You know what you are doing and what you want to do for the rest of your life. Go for it. We all know Jack wouldn't want anyone else to take over the nursery." Amelia says smiling at her sons and daughter in law.

****

"The wedding was beautiful, Jack. I wish you could have seen it in person." Austin says to his boss and owner of Stampley's Nursery where he worked while showing him photos from the wedding. "All of the flowers we did just made it more beautiful."

"I am so proud of what you did Austin. I have heard nothing but wonderful feedback from those that attended last week." Jack says to Austin. "You really are the best part of the nursery now that I am an old man."

"I was wondering what you thought about me buying it from you." Austin asks not sure how Jack would take it. "You have been gone so much lately anyways that it might be a relief to you."

"Austin, are you sure you would want the burden of it all on your shoulders? You are a young man and need to find a nice girl to settle down with and start a family."

"All I know is this nursery, Jack. I have worked here since I was young. I love this place already as if it were my own. You have taught me everything I know and wouldn't know what to do if I wasn't coming here every day."

"Your brother just married that Doone girl and is happily in love. Don't you want to find a girl to marry too? You aren't getting any younger."

"Easier said than done Jack. I would love to find a girl and settle down, but I just haven't found her yet." Austin says shaking his head knowing Jack will keep this subject up if he didn't find something to change it. "Don't you think I have been looking all these years?"

"What about Leah?"

"Your granddaughter? She hasn't been back here in years, why would you even bring her up?" Austin asks confused. He hadn't thought of Leah in years.

"I always thought you two would get together and make me a proud great-grandfather!"

"I'm sorry to burst your bubble or smash your lovely dream there Jack, but Leah and I don't even know each other that well and I haven't seen her in years. That is out of the question. Sorry old man."

"We will see about that young man." Jack whispers to himself and smiles while following Austin into the office.

Made in the USA
Coppell, TX
30 September 2020